THE PHANTOM FISHERBOY
Tales of Mystery and Magic

Ruth Ainsworth

THE PHANTOM FISHERBOY

Tales of Mystery and Magic

Illustrated by Shirley Hughes

André Deutsch

Books by the same author

THE TEN TALES OF SHELLOVER
MORE TALES OF SHELLOVER
THE PHANTOM CYCLIST
THE PHANTOM ROUNDABOUT
THE TALKING ROCK
THE MYSTERIOUS BABA AND HER MAGIC CARAVAN

First published October 1974 by
André Deutsch Limited
105 Great Russell Street London WC1
Second impression April 1977
Third impression March 1980

Printed in Great Britain by The Anchor Press Ltd
and bound by Wm Brendon & Son Ltd
both of Tiptree, Essex

ISBN 0 233 96569 6

First published in the United States of America 1980

*Library of Congress Number
79 92493*

Contents

The Phantom Fisherboy

Greenlees Comprehensive School, in spite of its pleasant name, was in the heart of a city. It was a grimy, red brick building, with high, narrow windows that the children couldn't possibly see out of, and a sloping, concrete playground that grazed the children's knees when they fell. But most of the pupils thought it the best school in the world, and were certain that the head, Mr Felling, was the best headmaster.

Mr Felling was tall and thin, with a mop of untidy white hair, and he seemed always to be planning surprises for the children. Barry had been at the school for less than a year, but already he had visited a museum and a theatre and a factory. Now, in the summer term, his class were going into the country to stay for a week in a little village, to study village life.

Most of the class had never been to a proper village with cobbled streets and an old church and one village shop which sold everything from shoelaces to sherbet.

Mrs Corbett, their form mistress, told them what to expect and recommended Wellingtons and a thick jersey. They were to stay in an old Manor house that had been made into a Field Study Centre. Other children would be staying there from other schools, studying other subjects, such as birds or pond life or farming.

Barry felt almost sick with excitement when the coach drove off, with Mrs Corbett and the whole class inside. Their luggage was on the rack and they each had a brand new note-

7

book where they could jot down anything special they passed on the way. A young master, Mr Spens, was with them as well. Everyone was laughing and talking at the top of their voices, but they grew quieter as they left the city behind.

Some boys noted down the lorries and tankers they passed. Others the bridges they crossed. Barry always looked eagerly at any rivers or canals, and hoped he might see someone fishing on the bank. It was his great ambition to go fishing, though he did not know how he would ever manage it. A home-made net and a jam jar and the chance of some tiddlers from the pond in the park was the nearest he had got to fulfilling his dream.

They stopped for drinks and ate their sandwiches at a motorway café. Then, before tea, they arrived at Rokeby Manor.

The Field Study Centre was vast and Barry felt nervous about finding his way. He was in a bedroom with seven other boys and after tea he felt more at home, having found his way successfully to the dining-room and back again.

The first morning he woke up early, though they had all been a long time getting to sleep the evening before. They had lain awake talking and eating sweets till Mr Spens had explained how many other children there were wanting to get to sleep, and that they must be quiet.

'You can talk your heads off tomorrow,' he said, 'unless you're working so hard that you haven't the time to speak.'

'We're not going to do proper lessons, are we, Sir?'

'Lessons of a sort but not the sort you're used to. You may all wish yourselves back at Greenlees.'

'Oh no, Sir, we won't!'

Barry tip-toed to the window and looked out. The river ran near by, winding through green fields, glowing and glinting in the morning sun. There were black and white cows in the meadows. Then, at the bend nearest the Manor, he saw a boy, standing alone on the bank. He was fishing.

Barry could not distinguish his face, but he could see that he was about his own size, wearing peculiar trousers that seemed to button below the knee. His jacket had a belt, which was odd, and he wore a cap on the back of his curly head. He had a fishing basket on the grass beside him. He cast his line very skilfully and when Barry saw him reel in and take something leaping and silvery off the hook, he felt a surge of excitement. The boy put the fish in the basket and quickly cast again.

Barry got dressed quietly and stole downstairs without meeting anybody. The other children seemed to be still asleep, though there was a bustle in the big kitchen. The front door stood wide open and he stepped outside into the fresh, blue morning.

It did not take many minutes to cross the garden, open a little, white gate, and follow the track to the river, but when he reached the place where the river went round the bend, the bank was deserted. The boy had gone. There was just a patch of flattened grass where the fishing basket had rested, and marks in the dew where his feet had been.

Barry could not decide where the boy had gone. He hadn't crossed the Manor grounds, that was certain. And he wasn't anywhere along the river bank to the left. He rounded the bend and looked to the right, but in neither direction was there a person in sight. Just then he heard the clang-clang-clang of a bell.

'That may mean breakfast,' he thought, 'and I'm starving.' He raced back to the Centre, very glad to see bowls of steaming porridge and racks of toast, and to smell delicious bacon. He was glad to see bacon *and* eggs *and* fried bread on his plate, when he had finished his porridge,

Mr Spens was right. They did work hard. They worked all day. But it was so different and interesting that it felt more like a holiday. Some of the children drew a plan of the village. Others did brass-rubbings inside the church.

9

Some worked in the churchyard and drew tombstones and copied inscriptions. There was no end to the things they could do.

Barry chose to work in the churchyard and he drew the tombstone of a child. He had chosen it because he did not draw very well and the plain headstone looked simple. He

liked the words carved on the stone and copied them out. They read, under their covering of grey-green lichen:

> *Earth was a beauteous, shining place,*
> *Till death cut short my mortal race;*
> *So very sweet life seemed to me,*
> *I ask you, friends, to pray for me.*

The name of the boy was Thomas Treen and he was drowned when he was eleven years old.

'Same age as me,' thought Barry. 'Pity he didn't go to Greenlees Comprehensive. Mr Felling likes us all to learn to swim during our first year.' He himself could do a length breast stroke and he was going to float next.

After tea, there was cricket and rounders on the big lawn and a few boys kicked a football about. Barry went for a stroll with his friend Saul who was interested in fishing too, though only in theory. Like Barry, he had never, yet, held a rod in his hands. They saw several fish jumping and watched the circles spreading on the surface of the water. The midges were out, dancing in swarms, and nibbling their wrists and ankles. It was the hungry midges who eventually drove them indoors.

The next morning Barry woke early again. He crept to the window and was not surprised to see the lonely fisherboy as before, dressed in the same clothes and standing exactly in the same place. He shook Saul gently:

'Wake up, Saul.'

Saul murmured sleepily and then opened his eyes.

'Don't wake the others. I've something to show you out of the window.'

Saul padded to the window and looked out.

'Gosh, I wish I were fishing like that boy.'

'So do I. I saw him yesterday.'

'Shall we go and talk to him? He might let us hold his rod, or at least have a look at it. Doesn't he cast well?'

'Let's get dressed and go down there.'

They were dressed in two minutes and left the room quietly. They never wanted to get up early at home, but here it was different. It was hard to go to sleep in the country, but easy to wake up. The air was fresh and cool in their faces and the grass was soaking with dew under their gym shoes.

Both boys kept their eyes fixed on the fisherboy as they crossed the garden and went through the small white gate. When they reached the bend in the river, though they hadn't taken their eyes off him, he had vanished.

'Let's see if there is a gap in the hedge,' suggested Barry. 'There's no other way he could have gone.'

But though they walked up and down in both directions they didn't find a gap, or even a weak place where someone might have squeezed through.

'The same thing happened yesterday,' said Barry. 'I saw him from our window and I ran all the way from the Centre. But he was quicker than me.'

'Do you think he just – faded?' asked Saul.

'You mean like a ghost?'

'Yes, that's exactly what I mean.'

'I think he did.'

'You believe he wasn't real at all?'

Barry hesitated a moment. 'Yes, that's what I do believe. He had such funny clothes. That queer, belted jacket and that cap. No one wears a cap.'

'And those long shorts. Or maybe short long trousers. They seemed to button below his knees.'

'I think he had boots on.'

'He didn't seem to belong.'

'That's what I thought,' agreed Barry.

'I wonder if he showed himself just to us?' Saul sounded puzzled.

'No, he couldn't possibly have known that I would look

out of my window yesterday and that we'd both look out today. Now could he?'

'I believed he was just enjoying himself fishing early on a sunny morning.'

'Yesterday I saw him catch a fish, remember.'

'Then if he's a ghost, was the fish real?'

Saul's question was almost impossible to answer and the breakfast bell rang before they'd decided whether it was a real fish or a ghostly one.

The third morning was misty, a beautiful, white mist such as the boys had never seen in the city. It reached only a few feet above the ground and the tops of the trees were in clear air.

'It looks as if the trees were wading,' said one of the girls.

Barry and Saul thought it was too misty for fishing, and anyhow they had slept late. 'It'll be clear in an hour,' said Mr Spens, and so it was. The sun shone brilliantly and the river sparkled. That day was spent on a neighbouring farm where they helped the farmer. Some of them sketched the well and the byre. There was a small, round building with a pointed roof called the gin-gang. Here, in olden times, a horse had gone round and round and round working some machinery that had threshed the grain. Barry felt sorry for the horse.

The next morning was spent in writing up anything they hadn't had time to draw or describe earlier on. Barry found an old skewer and cleaned up the lettering on Thomas Treen's tomb. It was much easier to read when he had finished. He felt pleased.

While he was finishing the work, an old lady came through the churchyard on her way to the church. She was carrying a big bunch of flowers to put on the altar. Barry had already noticed the two brass vases full of roses that were shedding their petals. She stopped beside him and watched him work.

'I'm only cleaning up the letters a bit,' he explained a little anxiously. 'Then people can read the poem. It's a very nice poem.'

'What an excellent idea,' said the old lady. 'I knew Tommy Treen. He lived next door. I was only a wee bairn, but he played with my brothers.'

'Where was he drowned?' asked Barry.

'In the river – our river – at the bend below Rokeby Manor, where the current is strong. He had a new rod and he somehow let it slip. He tried to reach it and he fell in. It was early in the morning and no one saw him or heard him cry out. No one could save him.'

'Pity he couldn't swim,' said Barry.

'Yes, it was. None of us village children could swim a stroke. His mother gave the new rod to my brother Ned who had been his best friend. He's dead now and I've got the rod in my attic. It's doing no good up there except gathering dust. Do you like fishing?'

Barry had quite lost his shyness and he told the old lady of his longing to fish and how he hoped, one day, he could have a try.

'So far I've only caught tiddlers in a jam jar,' he explained. 'But one day I'll catch a real fish.'

'What will you do with it?'

'My mum'll cook it for my tea and I'll give the head and the tail to our cat, Tiger.'

'If I gave you the rod, would your parents allow you to fish somewhere near your home?'

'Oh yes, sure they would. There's only the canal but dad would take me. Or maybe I can go alone now I can swim two lengths.'

'Come and fetch the rod before you leave for home. I live at the end cottage facing the green. I must go and do the flowers now.'

Barry explained to Mrs Corbett that he'd been given a

fishing rod by an old lady and she said it would be all right to take it. On the last evening, after tea, he went round to the old lady's cottage. She had the rod all ready in the hall. And a wicker fish basket.

'Here you are, Barry. I wondered if you'd like the fish basket as well? It belonged to Tommy too.'

'Oh, thank you, very very much. Can you spare it?'

'Of course I can. I haven't used the basket for years, not since I took my cat, Minty, to the vet to have her ear dressed.'

Barry had the rod in one hand and the basket in the other. But he was in no hurry to go.

'Do you think people – or children – come back to earth after they are dead?'

The old lady looked at him with bright, kind eyes.

'So you've seen Tommy, too, have you?'

'Yes. Several times. Always before breakfast, fishing at the bend where he fell in. Have you seen him?'

'Yes, often when I was younger. My eyes don't see so clearly now. He so loved fishing. My brother used to go with him. I suppose he was so happy that he couldn't, quite, forsake the river bank when he went away. There's so much we don't understand. Remember the line on his tomb:

So very sweet life seemed to be.

Perhaps it was too sweet to cut himself off from it for ever.'

'Ghosts only come back to places where they were happiest, maybe,' said Barry. 'I'd like to believe that. It doesn't seem so creepy and sad.'

'Well, let's believe that, you and I, shall we?'

Barry still lingered, unwilling to go.

'Do you think he needs his rod and his basket? Can he use them if I take them miles away?'

'My dear, I'm sure he'll find a ghostly rod and basket to hand when necessary. No, you won't rob him. He's beyond

material things now, poor lad. Such a beautiful boy, I remember. Such thick curly hair.'

Barry took the greatest care of his new treasures in the coach. He laid them carefully on the rack and kept looking up at them. He longed to use his new rod with its whippy end and its racketty wheel, that clicked as it turned.

Later in the year, fishing in the grimy canal, he had his first catch and laid it in the wicker basket.

Shadowy Paws

I am Belinda, the house cat. I am black and white, with gooseberry-green eyes, and though I am not a Persian, my tail is fluffy and I have a becoming ruff round my neck. I didn't really know what I looked like till a few months ago when a handsome ginger tom asked if he could be my mate. He was continually praising my green eyes and my fluffy tail and my delicate paws.

I am feeling restless today because my kittens will soon be born. They are my very first kittens. I know just what to do, but I do wish my mate took more interest in the coming event. After all, they are his children as well as mine.

I can't decide exactly where to have them. My mistress has made up her mind where *she* wants the nursery to be. She has put a carton lined with newspaper and a soft piece of blanket under the kitchen table. It is very suitable, and yet . . . yet I feel restless. I've just done a tour of the whole house, except the rooms where the doors were shut. I've felt drawn to many places, though each has some drawback, too light, too exposed, too far from the kitchen and the back door. I've considered the eiderdown on the spare bed, my mistress's wardrobe and the airing cupboard.

Then I decided what to do. I would explore the wash-house which is a small, brick building outside the back door, with a red, tiled roof and a chimney. My mistress never uses it as she has an automatic washing machine. There's an old copper in the corner where, in olden times, the clothes were boiled on wash-day. A fire was lit in a grate

under the copper to heat the water. I'll have a last scout round and though I don't suppose it will be suitable, I must make sure. Then I'll decide between the eiderdown and the airing cupboard.

I went to the back door and mewed to be let out and my mistress opened the door at once. She seldom keeps me waiting, not even if I choose to go out and come back in several times. My master is not so patient. If he opens the door for me and I streak out, he usually says sharply: 'Go out and stay out. I've more important things to do than open and shut doors for you all day.'

I walked the few steps to the wash-house door and found it ajar. I squeezed through the crack with difficulty. As I went in, I saw the copper in the corner, the sink under the window, and the uneven flags on the floor. But I scarcely noticed these details as I was aware of a strange sound – a cat mewing. Sometimes the mews were sad and sometimes desperate. I felt the fur bristle along my spine. Could it be my mate, the ginger tom, come to visit me at last? But I had no hope as his voice is quite different, very vibrant and robust. This voice was feminine and full of heart-break.

I sniffed carefully round the little room, but smelt only damp and mould and a whiff of dead flowers. My fur stood on end and my heart raced. I knew there was a cat near by, invisible but present. I turned round several times, quickly, looking over my shoulder. Then, in the shadows I saw her.

She was standing at the foot of the old copper and I thought, at first, she was carrying something in her mouth, something soft, like a new-born kitten. Then her image became clearer and the kitten (if it were a kitten) disappeared. She was a very slender and graceful tortoiseshell, with pretty patches of jet black among the surrounding brown and orange and white. She was much too thin, undernourished, probably.

'Who are you?' I inquired politely.

'They call me Willow,' she replied. 'I used to live here, a long time ago. Sometimes I'm so sad that I cannot bear my grief in silence any longer, and I cry aloud. I'm very sorry if I've upset you. Please forget it. You'd think the passing

of the years would soften my sorrow. But it doesn't. Broken hearts never mend.'

'I've never caught even a glimpse of you before,' I said, 'and I'm always about the place, house or garden. I live here. I'm the house cat.'

'Haven't you guessed that I'm no longer a living cat?' said Willow. 'My fur holds no warmth. I can walk over dead, dry leaves and they never rustle. I'm a ghost.'

'I don't understand,' I said, bewildered. 'Can you move invisibly and pass through closed doors? I should find that gift very useful myself, at times.'

'I can do all the things you mention,' said Willow sadly, 'But I can never have a family of kittens and feed them and bring them up.'

'No doubt, when you were alive, you had many a delightful family?'

'Indeed I did,' said Willow, in a more cheerful voice. 'I find adding up tedious, but I've heard my mistress tell other people that I had had at least fifty kittens, each plump and perfect.'

'What put a stop to your happy, productive life?' I said. 'That is, if you can bear to speak of it to another cat. I, too, am shortly to give birth.'

'Your first?' inquired Willow.

'Yes, my very first.'

'I can assure you that it is a cat's crowning experience,' purred Willow. 'Nothing else in life compares with it. Do make yourself comfortable – perhaps on that sack? Standing is a strain in your condition. Is that better?' I nodded. 'Then I'll begin,' and Willow settled down herself with her front paws doubled under and her fine-pointed tail curled neatly round.

'Although I had had many families, I still felt restless when the birth drew near. Whatever spot I chose, my mistress always found me and carried me back into the

kitchen and put me gently in a basket with a soft piece of cloth inside, often an old vest. But on this occasion, I was wandering about the house, as I expect you have been doing, considering various cupboards and corners, when I suddenly remembered the wash-house. It was a very snug place then, often with a fire lit to heat the copper. It hadn't the damp, unpleasant smell it has now. I took a fancy to a wooden box where newspapers were stored for starting the copper fire. It was dry and draught proof. I knew I hadn't much time and I climbed inside. The kittens were born almost immediately.

'I heard my mistress calling me, but I did not answer, and she never thought to search the wash-house. When my master was locking-up for the night, he shut the door. No one knew I was there.

'The kittens' father was a wild, devil-may-care black cat, named Lochinvar. He was of Scottish descent, the most famous robber of larders and fish shops in the district. He had no home and lived rough, which suited him. He was black as night from nose to tail with not a white hair on him. The kittens were quite charming. One was pure tortoiseshell like me, one black like his father, and the third quite extraordinary, black with a collar of white. I'd never seen a cat marked in the same way.

'The kittens were vigorous and feeding well, when I smelt smoke and saw a glow on the floor, near the copper. The fire was raked out when the washing was done, and the cinders used again next time. A cinder must have remained, just glowing. The wind was getting up, I heard it in the cherry tree outside, and a draught was blowing under the door. This fanned the glow into a flame. The flames licked higher and a pile of dry wood caught fire. I heard the sticks crackling and snapping.

'I knew what danger we were in and I knew there was no time to spare. I ran to the door to make sure it was shut. It

22

was. I jumped on to the sink and up on to the window sill
and wondered if I could possibly break the glass, but that

did not seem likely. We were trapped, with the flames leaping
higher and higher and the smoke billowing around.

'There was only one possible way of escape. Up the
chimney. Seizing the tortoiseshell kitten in my mouth, as she
was the smallest, I pushed my way into the grate which

was still hot, but not uncomfortably so, and I started up the flue. I was nearly choked with soot and footholds were not easy to find, but somehow I managed it, and got out of the top of the chimney into the cold, starry night.

'The wash-house was a low building and I easily jumped to the ground, though carrying my kitten upset my balance and I jarred myself painfully in landing. I hadn't a moment to spare to search for a suitable place to leave the kitten. I simply dropped her on the mat outside the back door and went back. Slithering *down* the chimney was quick and easy compared with the slow climb up.

'I reached the newspaper box and took the white-collared kitten in my mouth. By this time I was coughing with the fumes but I knew exactly what I had to do and somehow I did it. The kitten was left with her sister on the mat.

'When I got the all-black kitten in my mouth I never imagined all would not go well. What I had done twice before, surely I could do again. But I hadn't bargained for the dense smoke that now made breathing impossible, and the fierce flames that were licking round the hearth. I smelt my fur singeing as I raced through and began my climb. I struggled for breath and scrambled frantically for footholds in the chimney. I don't remember much more. I must have perished, suffocated in the chimney. When I picked the kitten up I noticed he didn't mew or move, and he may well have been dead already. Such a fine son, he was. I had noticed and admired his broad forehead and the wide span of his paws, so like his father, Lochinvar.

'That is my story. Not a very cheerful one, I'm afraid, but you will soon have forgotten it when you have your own little ones. It's many years since a fire was lit under this old copper, but I don't recommend the wash-house for your first family. Has your mistress provided a bed for you?'

'Yes,' I said, 'under the kitchen table.'

'Very suitable. Use it, my dear. You'll find it a most con-

venient place, close to the back door for your own requirements, and also for the kittens when you take them out. Kittens need the company of human beings if they are to grow into contented house cats, and the kitchen is such a warm, suitable place.'

'There was one thing in your story that struck me as quite extraordinary,' I said. 'It was the black kitten with the pure white collar. I was told by my mother that *her* grandmother was pitch black with just such a collar. Could it be – do you think it possible – that you and I are related? I shall tell my kittens about your heroic action and I should like to tell them that you were one of their ancestors.'

'It is very likely,' said Willow. 'We may be blood relations though it seems odd to refer to a bloodless, shadowy creature like me in that way. This house has a tradition of cat-loving families and my surviving kittens were well brought up, though they were motherless. I occasionally managed to visit them. My mistress fed them from a doll's feeding bottle and even came downstairs each night to give them a night feed. I'm very grateful to her. She was almost cat-like in her devotion.'

'Are you happy now you're – now you're not alive?' I asked shyly.

'Now I'm a ghost, you mean? I'm not unhappy. I stay around this house and garden where I knew every smell, every nook and corner, every branch in the cherry tree, every blade of grass. I shall visit your kittens when they are born. You may not see me, but they will. Kittens with newly-opened eyes see many strange things. Now go and settle in your box under the table. You haven't long to wait.'

Willow sprang on to the copper and disappeared and I made my way slowly to the back door. My first mew brought my mistress to open it and I crept into my box. She stayed beside me for some time, stroking me and tickling me under the chin which she knew I found soothing.

An hour later my kittens were born, four beautiful children, two taking after their father and two after me. I was delighted to see that one of my three daughters was pure black with a white collar. I only hope she will grow up to have the courage and devotion of her heroic ancestor, Willow.

The Mascot

Mildred's father was a lorry driver. He was very large, with untidy black hair and an enormous laugh that made the cups and saucers rattle. He drove a very big lorry with twelve wheels.

Once, Mildred had gone for a ride with him in the cab, high up above the other cars, and she felt very important, and not very safe. She was too small to see properly through the windscreen and she felt helpless. Could they run over something or someone without knowing? Surely these heavy, double wheels could crush a person without even a tiny jolt?

She told her mother all this when she got home and her mother said it was nonsense.

'Daddy is so tall,' she explained, 'that he can see perfectly through the windscreen and his window. He's the safest driver in town and has lots of certificates to show for it. He drives more than a thousand miles every week, by day or night, in all sorts of weather, and he's never even run over a cat. Or scratched his vehicle. You're safer driving with your father than you are on your own feet. And don't you ever forget it!'

All the same, when he was driving on a long run at night, Mildred hoped he was safe. She thought of his strong headlights piercing the darkness.

'Supposing it's foggy, daddy. What then?'

'That's simple enough. I turn on my fog-lights, or else drive into the first lay-by and have a bit of shut-eye.'

One day, when Mildred was shopping with her mother, she

saw something she liked in the window of the newsagent's shop. It was a little gnome, dangling from a silver ribbon. His pointed hat was green. His jacket yellow with four green buttons. His trousers and his shoes red. His face was

white as paper with blobs of red on the cheeks, and a smiling red mouth with a neat white beard below.

Mildred stood and gazed at the gnome.

'Come on, child, I'll be late with the dinner.' Her mother sounded impatient.

'Let me look a little longer. I'll run and catch you up.'

'You've looked long enough. Your eyes'll drop out. Hurry up.'

She tugged at Mildred's hand and Mildred reluctantly let herself be dragged away.

The next morning she ran ahead so she could look at her dear little gnome, while her mother visited the butcher's and the grocer's, which were near by. She had never wanted anything as much in her life as she wanted the gnome. He looked back at her in a friendly way too. She thought he almost winked as if they shared a secret.

'Still staring, saucer-eyes,' said her mother. 'Whatever are you looking at? I suppose that fairy doll with her gauzy wings. I can tell you now, that all that silver will go black in no time. And it's 75p. Useless trash!'

'I haven't even *seen* a doll,' said Mildred, desperately. 'I'm looking at that lovely, lovely gnome.'

'Oh, that! Come along, do. You've had time to examine every blessed thing in the window. And that gnome isn't meant for a child. It isn't a toy.'

As they went home, her mother walking so fast that Mildred had to run to keep, she asked:

'What is it if it isn't a toy?'

'What is what?'

'The gnome. The lovely gnome.'

'Oh, that. It's a mascot. That's why it has a string to hang it up by.'

'What's a mascot?'

'Something that brings luck. Or is supposed to bring luck. Like the silver horseshoe someone gave your Aunt Belle at her wedding.'

'Does it bring everyone luck?'

'No, just the person it's given to. But I don't believe such nonsense. Black cats are supposed to be lucky and white heather and a wish-bone.'

'What do people do with mascots?'

'Carry them in their pocket or put them safe in a drawer. But that thing in the newspaper shop was meant to hang in a car.'

'I'd like to buy it. How much was it, mummy?'

'5op.'

'Can I have 5op?'

'No, you can't. It isn't your birthday.'

'I want to give it to daddy.'

'Well, I haven't 5op to waste on rubbish.'

'It isn't rubbish. It's a mascot. You said it was.'

'Stop whining. When you're a big girl and have a paper-round and earn money, you can buy what you like.'

That evening, Mildred's father was at home and she sat on his knee while he watched the telly and smoked his pipe. When he laughed, his whole body shook and she shook with it. She liked sharing his pleasure though her own eyes were usually tightly shut, so she never saw the screen.

'Daddy. Will you give me 5op?'

'What for, my little poppet?'

'For to buy you a present.'

'But I don't want a present.'

'Oh, but you don't have to want this one. You need it. I can't tell you why or it won't be a surprise.'

'You can have it if you can find 5op in my pocket.'

He brought out a great handful of money, coppers and silver, and Mildred soon picked out the 5op piece, with all its corners.

'Thank you, daddy.'

The next morning she was ready to go to the shops directly after breakfast.

'Come on, mummy,' she said impatiently.

'I must redd up the hearth and put these clothes to steep and wash the front step. Don't hurry me. Dust the stairs while you're waiting.'

Mildred had no liking for dusting, but she took the yellow duster and began. She did not get far, as a friend had shown her how to make a rabbit out of a handkerchief. She found she could make a better one out of the duster. At last they set out, Mildred holding the 5op piece tightly.

'Please, Mrs Stubbs, may I buy your gnome out of the window?'

Mrs Stubbs took the money and put the gnome in a striped paper bag. Her father seemed very pleased when she gave him his present.

'He'll bring you luck,' explained Mildred. 'You'll never have an accident or get lost or have a breakdown. He's a mascot. A good luck mascot.'

'That's just what I need,' said her father, kissing her. 'I'll hang him in my cab. What shall I call him?'

'His name is Tom Thumb.'

So Tom Thumb was hung in the cab of the lorry and he swung and swayed as it rumbled along.

A few days later, when her father came home, Mildred was in bed, but not asleep. When he had had his tea, he came up to say good night.

'A funny thing happened to me today,' he said, sitting down on her bed so that all the springs squeaked. 'I stopped at the Scots Roundabout for petrol, as I've done many a time, and I got out to stretch my legs. It's all built up round there and blow me if I didn't see a garden gnome in one of the houses exactly like Tom Thumb. Exactly. I see the little chap so often that I know just what he's like, green hat, yellow jacket, red trousers and shoes. Wasn't it odd?'

'What was the garden gnome doing, daddy?'

'Nothing. Leastwise he was standing in the middle of a tiny front lawn no bigger than our table.'

'What was he made of?'

'I don't know. Plaster, perhaps.'

'Tom Thumb is soft and cuddly. I think he's stuffed with cotton wool. Plaster could break, but Tom Thumb couldn't.'

'He could burn,' said her father.

'Daddy, don't say such horrid things. He wouldn't be lucky if he got burned, would he? He wouldn't be a proper good luck mascot.'

A week later, Mildred's father came into the kitchen carrying Tom Thumb.

'Look, mother,' he said. 'I've somehow got a great dirty smudge right in the front of the little fellow's yellow coat. Can't think how. Get it out for me, will you?'

Mildred's mother took a bottle of grease remover and damped a cloth and rubbed the smear for several minutes, round and round.

'It's getting worse, not better. I'll try strong detergent.'

She dipped the cloth in some hot, foaming water and tried again. But for all her efforts the mark looked worse, not better.

They tried soda and vinegar and lemon juice, but nothing was any good.

'He's just as lucky with a dirty coat as a clean one,' said her father. 'Like I love you just as much with a jammy mouth as a clean one.'

Mildred quickly wiped her mouth on the towel.

So Tom Thumb went back to his place in the cab with his dirty yellow jacket.

A few nights later, Mildred's father came home while she was having her hair washed. Her mother had finished rubbing it and was trying to comb out the tangles. She had dark hair like her father. She hated this part and was apt to complain loudly that her mother was pulling and hurting.

'Stay still, missy,' said her father. 'I've something to tell you you'll like to hear.'

'Is it about Tom Thumb?'

'Yes and no. Well, I stopped for petrol again at Scots Roundabout and I got out as usual to stretch my legs. I looked at the garden gnome, just to check he was still there, and blow me, if he hadn't a great black mark right in the middle of his yellow jacket! I could hardly believe my eyes. It was remarkable seeing a gnome dressed like Tom Thumb, but to see one with a dirty coat as well – I was fair bewildered.'

'Daddy, what does it mean? Tell me what it means? Tell me why they'd both got the same mark?'

Her father was silent, but her mother answered quickly.

'Don't be so daft, the pair of you. What does it mean, indeed! It doesn't mean a thing, except that the garden gnome got some dirt on him. A naughty boy might have smeared some earth on him for fun. Don't make mysteries out of nothing.'

33

Mildred and her father did not reply. No one likes to be called 'daft'.

For several weeks Mildred always asked her father if he had been to Scots Roundabout, but the answer was always no. His work had taken him north, not south. The only thing that happened to Tom Thumb was that he lost one of his green buttons, the top one.

'It's somewhere in the cab,' said her father. 'I'll have a good turn out when I've got time and I'll find it. It must be somewhere, for sure, and your mother can sew it on.'

'Time you learned to sew it on yourself,' said her mother.

One day, Mildred's father said he was going past Scots Roundabout again.

'You'll look at the garden gnome, daddy?'

'Yes, unless I'm pushed for time. I'll look.'

Her father was to be away for two days as he was taking a load to Wales and bringing another back. He was often away a night and Mildred always missed him. He sometimes read her a story in bed, and he liked playing 'snap' almost as much as she. And he minded just as much when he lost. Her mother used to say crossly:

'Give over, do. What does it matter who said "snap" first? Put it in the pool. I don't know who is the biggest baby!'

When her father came back from Wales, Mildred could see at once that he had something to tell them. He was restless and couldn't settle down.

'What's up?' asked his wife.

'I've something to tell Mildred. To tell you both. And I don't know where to begin.'

'Then begin by having your tea. I've cooked three herrings for you. They're nice and fresh.'

He ate the herrings quickly and drank his mug of tea. Then he pushed his chair back. Mildred had never taken her eyes off him since he had come in. She sat with her elbows

on the table, watching his face. Even her mother was sitting with her hands in her lap and hadn't picked up her knitting.

'It was like this,' began her father. 'I got caught in the rush hour and I didn't get moving till I was on the motorway. There was patchy fog that got worse as I went on. It blew right across the road and then cleared, so sometimes visibility was nil and the next minute quite good. But I could keep going, cautious like. I kept for some miles behind a tanker. I could see his tail-light glowing red. I followed him right to Scots Roundabout. There I drew in and stretched my legs. My eyes smarted a bit with the fog and I had a cup of tea at the café next door.'

'And you looked at the garden gnome?' put in Mildred.

'Yes, I looked at the garden gnome like I said I would. The fog had cleared just then or I mightn't have bothered. There he was, just the same, with the same dirty smudge on his jacket. And I noticed something else. He had lost a top button, too. He had only three.'

'But a plaster gnome couldn't have buttons sewn on his front?' said his wife sharply.

' 'Course not, but he had them painted on. And one had gone. I tell you, the top one just wasn't there! I didn't think, I just walked up the path and knocked on the door. It was very neglected, with the paint peeling off the wood, and long grass was growing round the gnome. There was rubbish lying around, paper and a broken milk bottle. I saw a postman and asked him who lived there. He said an old man had lived there once, but he wasn't there now. The place was empty. He said no one would live there again because the row was to be pulled down and shops built.

'I nearly brought the gnome away with me as no one rightly owned it now, but I left it where it was. I didn't like to touch it.

'I drove off and after about five miles I saw red lights and accident signs and masses of police cars. There were ambu-

lances and a fire-engine. Traffic was all diverted, from both lanes. Before I turned back, I hung about a bit to see what had happened. The tanker I'd been following, and would still have followed if I hadn't stopped to look at the gnome, was carrying acid. An articulated lorry came up behind and tried to overtake. The fog must have been bad just then and he didn't see how close he was. He hit the back corner of the tanker and ten tons of acid gushed out on to the road and spilt over both carriageways. The driver of the lorry was killed and other people died of burns. I don't know how many. Perhaps we'll hear on the news.'

He turned on the transistor and a voice said:

This morning in bad visibility, there was a collision on the A1 between a tanker carrying 12 tons of acid and an articulated lorry. The driver of the lorry was killed outright. Three other people died of burns. Seventeen more are in hospital. There was a pile up of eight vehicles. The police cleared the north-bound carriageway by 6.0 p.m but the south-bound carriageway may be blocked for a further twelve hours. Drivers are advised . . .

'Your little Tom Thumb saved my life,' said her father. 'He really brought me luck. And so did his double, the garden gnome. It was the best 50p you ever spent, Mildred.'

'You don't *know* you'd have been in the pile-up,' said his wife. 'You might have been, just as I might have been in that bus that hit a lamp standard the other day. But I wasn't.'

'Likely I would have been,' said her husband. 'I was driving fairly close to the tanker to keep within sight of his rear light. I doubt whether I could have pulled up inside yards. I'd have been for it. I've had a narrow escape.'

Mildred felt excited and relieved and puzzled all at the same time. But she had no doubt that Tom Thumb had saved

her father from a horrible accident. She didn't know how, but she knew he had done it.

Months later, in the summer, her father took them all for a holiday in Wales and on the way he promised to let her see the garden gnome at Scots Roundabout. He had bought a little red Ford and they sped along the motorway under a cloudless blue sky. They stopped at the café at the Roundabout for a drink, but Mildred begged to be shown the garden gnome first. They walked a few yards to the row of little houses, now mostly empty, but not yet pulled down. They stopped by the second one.

'He was here,' said her father.

'But he isn't now. He's gone. Let's see if there are any pieces left behind.'

The three of them examined the broken milk bottle and an ice-cream carton and other litter. But that was all. Mildred was bitterly disappointed.

'We've still got Tom Thumb,' said her father cheerfully. 'Will you have a milk-shake or a still lemonade?'

'A raspberry milk-shake, please.'

Years later, when Mildred was grown up and had even out-grown her paper-round, the flavour of raspberry reminded her of that sunny morning and the sadness she felt when she knew she would never see the garden gnome; all mixed up with the relief that they were all three together and safe.

Tom Thumb had to have a new jacket, it got so shabby, and his feet were ragged from banging against the windscreen. But by this time, Mildred was old enough, and clever enough, to make him some little red shoes herself.

The Invisible Rope

Suma was a little black girl and she lived in the jungle in a mud hut. The children in the village played among the mud huts where the grass was worn away and there was just earth left. In the dry season the earth was hard and dusty under their bare feet. In the rainy season it was covered with sticky mud.

Sometimes Suma and her friends went a little way into the jungle, but not very far. There was danger in the jungle, lions and elephants and snakes. Suma did not want to be eaten by a lion or crushed by an elephant or bitten by a snake. The jungle was dark and narrow paths led under trees hung with creepers and ferns. There was always a noise going on, the chattering of monkeys or the screaming of parrots.

Wherever Suma went she carried her wooden doll, Teg, with her. Teg wore no clothes, just a necklace of beads. She was hard and brown and had a sharp nose jutting out of a flat face. Suma thought she was very beautiful and she told her everything.

Beyond the village, quite by itself, was the hut of the Ju-ju man. The Ju-ju man could make magic and people were afraid of him. He could cure people of sickness, but he could make them sick too. He could find lost things, but he could also make things disappear. He could bring anyone good luck, but he could also bring them bad luck.

People kept away from the Ju-ju man unless they wanted to ask his advice about something. Then they always brought

him a present, some feathers or a fish or a string of beads. The Ju-ju man liked his presents. His hut was full of curious and beautiful things that had been given him.

In the doorway of his hut hung a curtain of beads, threaded in long strings. Suma often went past his hut so that she could stare at this bead curtain. It must have taken hundreds and hundreds of beads, and it must have taken the Ju-ju man days and days to thread them.

Sometimes the bead curtain left a little peep-hole and Suma liked to look through. The Ju-ju man was always doing something interesting. He might be reading one of his big books, or painting yellow streaks on his black face. He might be cooking and stirring his big black pot with a wooden spoon. Sometimes he was pounding up roots and leaves to make magic medicines.

One day, when Suma crept close to the bead curtain, she heard a soft, snorting sound. It was the Ju-ju man snoring. She peeped inside and had a good look at him. He was lying on a mat on the floor, with a red blanket over him and his head on a feather pillow. She could see one skinny foot poking out, and a skinny hand. The hut smelt nice because there were bunches of dried plants hanging from the roof. They smelt of peppermint and other spicy things.

Suma crept on tip-toe into the hut and began to look round. There was a snakeskin and a fan of plumy feathers, and a set of bowls made of clay. There were many other things and Suma looked at them all. The Ju-ju man never moved and he never opened his eyes.

There was a bowl of something standing beside the Ju-ju man in case he felt thirsty. Suma was feeling thirsty herself, and she knelt down and smelt the bowl. It smelt like straw-berries. Then she put a finger in and licked it. It tasted like strawberries. Then she put Teg on the floor and picked up the bowl and had a drink. Then she had another – and another – and another till the bowl was empty.

As she put the empty bowl back the Ju-ju man sprang off the mat and glared at her. He looked very frightening with

streaks of yellow paint on his face, and on his head a hat made of monkey tails. She clutched Teg more tightly.

'Who drank my strawberry drink?' he said.

'I did,' said Suma.

'Why did you drink it?'

'Because I was thirsty.'

Suma tried to move nearer to the bead curtain because she wanted to slip out and run home, but her feet would not move a step.

'You are in my power,' said the Ju-ju man. 'I shall keep you here to be useful to me.'

'But I'm not very useful,' said Suma.

'You will be useful to me. Can you sing?'

'Yes,' said Suma.

'Then you can sing me to sleep. Can you dance?'

'Yes,' said Suma.

'Then you can dance for me when I want to be amused. And when I don't want to be sung to, or danced to, you can dust my belongings with this little feather duster.'

'I don't think I want to sing, or dance, or dust your belongings,' said Suma.

'Well, you must do it whether you want or not. It is a great honour to work for an important person like myself. If you are a lazy girl, I shall just change you into something really useful, like a broom or a pudding basin.'

Suma tried again to move but she could only take a step. There was something pulling at her ankle though she could see nothing when she looked down.

'Ha! Ha!' laughed the Ju-ju man. 'I've tied an invisible rope to your ankle so you can't run away. Wait, I'll make the rope a little longer.' He stooped down and made some movements in the air. 'Now you can go all over the hut and you can dance as well. But you can't get out of the hut. The rope isn't long enough.'

Suma pulled and tugged and pulled and tugged till her ankle was sore. But the rope would not give way. The Ju-ju man watched her and laughed.

'Silly child, stop pulling and tugging. It is a magic rope and even an elephant couldn't break it. Content yourself

41

here with me. Now I'm going to make some broth and you can stir it while it cooks. I like my broth well stirred.'

So Suma stopped struggling and stirred the broth in the big black pot. She held Teg in one hand and the spoon in the other. The Ju-ju man poured out a bowlful each and they sat and drank it. Suma sat on a little stool and the Ju-ju man sat on a bigger one. They ate some purple berries and the Ju-ju man said :

'I want to be amused. Dance to me.'

Suma knew a number of dances because the people in the village had a special dance for the full moon, for the harvest, for the rain and for many other occasions. Before she had danced them all the Ju-ju man gave a great yawn.

'Sing to me,' he said. 'I'm getting sleepy.'

This was easy as the people in the village had a special song for morning and evening, and before they went out hunting, and when they came home from hunting. Suma sang the one the mothers sing to their babies when they put them to bed.

> *The boat is rocking on the lake,.*
> *Only the owlets and frogs are awake,*
> *Rock with the boat,*
> *Rock high, rock low,*
> *Into the darkness of sleep you go.*

She had sung it only twice through when the Ju-ju man fell fast asleep.

He had made her a little bed in the corner with a striped blanket to wrap herself in, and she and Teg made themselves comfortable under it. Suma had decided to cry all night, but she was so sleepy that she went straight to sleep.

The days went by, and Suma lived in the hut with the Ju-ju man. He was often out, gathering plants to make magic with, and when he was in he was often busy, drying and rubbing and chopping and soaking the plants. There were jars and

jars of medicines on the shelf, and leaves folded into small green pill boxes.

Some of the village people came for advice, but Suma dared not try to attract their attention in case the Ju-ju man turned her into something really useful, like a broom. The Ju-ju man parted the bead curtain and went outside to give advice, and he came into the hut later with a gift. If it was good to eat he shared it with Suma.

When the Ju-ju man was out in the jungle, gathering plants, Suma talked to Teg. Teg never answered, but it was nice to talk to someone. One day, the Ju-ju man left her some stew for her dinner, and when she had eaten what she wanted she gave a spoonful to Teg. To her surprise, Teg ate it and smiled and said:

'Drink, please.'

So Suma gave her some water which she swallowed, and smiled again and said:

'Now I can talk as well as listen.'

'I never knew you could talk,' said Suma.

'Of course I can talk. As well as you or better. But I couldn't start till I'd had a bite and a sup. Let's make plans for our escape.'

'Yes, let's. What shall we do?'

'We can't escape till we have cut the invisible rope round your ankle.'

'But if it's invisible how can we cut it?'

'We shall have to learn some magic.'

'How can we unless the Ju-ju man teaches us, and he wont do that!'

'We must learn some ourselves from one of his big books.'

They took down one of his big books and began to study it. There were pictures on every page but the words were meaningless. Only little black marks on the page. They were studying the book so hard that they never heard the Ju-ju

man's footsteps. The first sound they noticed was the jingle of the bead curtain as the Ju-ju man came through, his monkey tails swinging up and down with rage.

'How dare you touch my books!' he said. 'I've a good mind to change you into a blade of grass and use you as a marker!'

'I'm doing no harm,' said Suma. 'I'm looking at the pictures and pretending to read to Teg. Of course I can't read but I make up stories for her. It passes the time when you are away.'

'Very well,' said the Ju-ju man, and he stopped shaking his monkey tails. 'Looking at the pictures will do you no harm. And making up stories for that poor dumb wooden creature will do you no harm either. You can look at my books when I am out if you wash your hands first, and always lay the book on a mat and not on the bare floor.'

Day after day Suma and Teg studied the book but they did not even begin to read. They did not even know their letters. Then, one morning, a red and black parrot flew through the bead curtain and began to talk.

'What are you two doing?' he said.

'How did you learn to talk?' said Suma.

'Years ago I lived in a cage in a house full of people. I soon learned their language, and I find I haven't forgotten it.'

He put his head on one side and rattled off:

'Polly! Pretty polly! Good boy! Naughty boy! Give him a lump of sugar.'

'It's very clever of you to talk so well.'

'That's nothing,' said the parrot. 'I can read too.'

'You can read!' said Suma and Teg together.

'The children in my house went to school and they did their lessons at the table over which my cage was hanging. Stupid little things they were, too. C-A-T spells cat. D-O-G spells dog. Over and over again. I learned to read and spell in no time.'

44

'Dear, clever, wonderful parrot, will you please read to us?'

'Some other time – some other time. The Ju-ju man may be home any minute, and I don't trust him. I have a horrid feeling that the fan over there is made of parrot feathers, so I'll be off.'

'Come back tomorrow! Come back tomorrow!' cried Suma, as the parrot spread his wings and flew off.

Suma and Teg could not sleep that night for thinking of the parrot, and wondering whether he would come back the next day. When the Ju-ju man had gone out, Teg thoughtfully hid the fan made of parrot feathers so it could not hurt his feelings. Then they waited.

The parrot soon appeared, and though he was ready and willing to read any page for them, there were so many pages that were not helpful.

'How to stop nose bleeding,' read the parrot.

'How to make hair grow.'

'How to get rid of ants.'

'Try to find something about an invisible rope,' begged Suma.

'How to make yourself invisible,' read the parrot.

'How to stop a baby from crying.'

'How to find a lost ring.'

'Look for the word rope,' said Suma, 'or is it too difficult?'

This hurt the parrot's pride as he could spell words with ten or twelve letters in them, let alone easy ones with only four. But they stroked his angry feathers till they lay flat again, and persuaded him to read on.

'How to make rope,' read the parrot.

'How to tie rope!'

'How to cut an invisible rope.'

Suma threw her arms round the parrot's neck and buried her face in his feathery ruff.

'Read on,' she said. 'Read on from there.'

The parrot gave a little cough to clear his throat, and read on:

'This can only be done at midnight when there is no moon.

Use a knife which has been washed in water, waved in air, rubbed with earth, and heated with fire.'

Before any more could be read, the parrot flew silently away as the Ju-ju man came in.

'People are so stupid,' he said, as he put on the broth. 'I had to turn two into turtles and one into a humming bird. I'm quite tired with making so much magic. I think I'll have a little nap while the broth is cooking. Don't stop stirring for a single minute. I shall ask the wooden spoon if you have been lazy when I wake up.'

'Teg,' whispered Suma. 'You stir while I get the knife ready.'

She found a knife with an ivory handle and washed it in water, waved it in air, rubbed it with earth, and then heated it in the flames under the pot. She hid it in her striped blanket.

The Ju-ju man woke up and shouted to the wooden spoon: 'Have you been stirring all the time?'

'Every minute, master. Every minute I stirred.'

When the broth was eaten the Ju-ju man did not want to be amused. He only wanted to go to sleep. So Suma sang her lullaby and he dropped off at once.

'How shall we know when it's midnight?' asked Suma.

'When the white owl screeches,' said Teg.

They lay listening to all the sounds of the jungle, branches creaking, frogs croaking, and soft paws padding. Then shrill and harsh, came the cry of the white owl.

Suma jumped out of bed, felt the place round her ankle where the invisible rope was tied, and struck with the knife. In a moment she was free. She could go where she wanted. With a last look round the dark hut, she tucked Teg under one arm, snatched the Ju-ju man's monkey tail hat from the peg where he hung it at night, and slipped through the bead curtain.

She ran to her own hut which was so different from the hut of the Ju-ju man. No rugs or fans or stools or books, but father and mother, grandfather and grandmother, and six brothers and sisters. Everyone woke up and had to be hugged and kissed, and all this hugging and kissing made them so hungry that Suma's mother made a batch of pancakes. How surprised they were when Teg ate a bit of pancake and had a sip of tea and said:

'Thank you very much.'

After this, Suma never went near the hut of the Ju-ju man, and when she saw him coming she hid behind a tree, or in

some suitable place. If he caught her, he would surely turn her into something useful, like a broom or a pudding basin.

As for the monkey tail hat, her father wore it when he wanted to look grand, at weddings and parties and feasts.

Sleep Well

'What are you going to do to-day?' said their uncle, looking at Paul and Harriet from under very bushy, black eyebrows.

'They'll find enough to interest them around the farm,' said their aunt. 'There's the pigs and calves and ducks and hens, all new to town children.'

'Is there a bull?' asked Harriet, who knew that bulls could be fierce. 'Will he mind my red hair-band?'

'We haven't a bull,' said their uncle. 'Nothing but the mildest cows. I suppose you're scared of them, seeing as you're not used to beasts.'

'I'm not,' said Harriet firmly.

'She isn't,' said Paul at the same time.

'Well, go out and enjoy yourselves. Can you both swim?'

'Yes,' said Paul.

'Ten strokes,' said Harriet.

'Then you can fall in the pond, if you like.'

Their uncle went off to his work and the children put on their boots. It was April and still cold, but the sun was shining. Their aunt was more helpful.

'Go where you like, my dears. You'll see the farm buildings wherever you go, now the trees are bare. You might like to play in the Round Wood.'

'Yes please,' said Paul and Harriet together. 'Where is it?'

'Go straight up the fields and keep by the hedge and you'll come to it.'

'Might we get lost?' asked Harriet.

'No, child. It's not big enough. It's more like a copse than a wood. Now run away. I'm going to make a beefsteak and kidney pie for dinner.'

They walked up three sloping fields and soon saw the wood. It didn't look particularly round. It didn't look very big, either. There was a path leading in which they followed.

Considering its size, the wood was full of interesting things. There was a deep ditch round the edge with a wooden plank for people to walk across. The plank was old and worn, but could be bounced on pleasantly. They hadn't gone far before Harriet saw a squirrel sitting on the ground, grubbing at the roots of a tree.

'Look, Paul!'

'I say, isn't he small and thin. I thought squirrels were round and plump.'

'He's been sleeping all the winter and not eating. Look, he's disappeared up that tree.'

'He's gone.'

'No, he's jumped right into the next tree.'

They watched till all that could be seen of the squirrel was a trail of shaking branches.

The birds were busy too, darting in and out of the bushes and twittering. One was carrying something in his beak which looked like wool.

'He's building his nest and lining it with sheeps' wool,' said Harriet. 'Oh Paul, wouldn't it be wonderful if we actually found a nest with eggs in it, like children do in books?'

'We'll find lots before we go home, I promise you. We've two whole weeks to look for them.'

'Isn't it lovely with only us,' said Harriet.

'Us and that girl.'

'What girl?'

'I saw her ahead of us before we crossed the plank. She must be somewhere in the wood.'

'Was she little?'

'Bigger than us, I think. Look, there she is again. Through the trees!'

Harriet looked where he pointed and saw a girl ahead, dressed in brown. She seemed to be wearing rather odd clothes, like a cloak. Then they lost sight of her.

The children followed the path till they reached the middle of the wood. Then suddenly, they found themselves in a clearing. It was quite different from the rest of the wood. The ground was uneven, covered with fine grass of a curiously bright green.

'How odd,' said Paul. 'I wonder why they cut the trees down just here.'

'There aren't any tree-stumps.'

'No, that's odd too.'

'Paul, that girl is watching us. Turn round and you'll see her.'

Paul turned quickly and saw the girl standing by a tree, her face deathly white. She was wrapped in a brown cloak. She disappeared from sight as he watched.

'Do you think she wants to be friends, Paul?'

'No, I think she was scared stiff. Did you see how pale she was?'

'But no one would be scared of us. We're only children.'

'She was though. Perhaps this wood is really private. I suppose it belongs to Uncle Jim. Perhaps she's been told never to come this way.'

'I know. Like:

> *My mother said, I never should,*
> *Play with the gipsies in the wood.'*

'We don't look in the least like gipsies. I rather wish we did. We have proper shoes and we're not brown enough.'

They played in the wood a little while, climbing about in a fallen tree. The brown girl didn't reappear and they soon forgot about her.

After they had their dinner, their aunt took them to the village shop to spend their pocket money. There was only one shop, but it sold almost anything anyone could want. They bought picture post cards to send to their parents, and Paul bought himself some marbles. Harriet chose a dolls' teaset. They played with their purchases on the hearth rug, which was made of hundreds of little snippets of material. The farm kitten, Polly, played too. She lapped milk out of one of Harriet's tiny saucers and chased Paul's marbles.

'I shall draw a plan of the Round Wood for my holiday task,' said Paul.

'What holiday task? I haven't got one,' said Harriet.

'Our form master says we're all to do a plan of something, preferably something out of doors. He suggested a park or a playground. But I shall do the Round Wood.'

'You can borrow my crayons if you like. My browns are jolly good. Better than yours.'

'Thank you. We'll go to the wood again tomorrow and I'll jot down a few things.'

'I may do a plan as well. Just for fun.'

The next morning they fed calves and collected eggs and helped their uncle, but after dinner they went off to the Round Wood

'There she is again,' said Paul, catching a glimpse of the girl in brown.

'She's beckoning.'

'No, she isn't.'

'Well, we're going that way anyhow.'

When they reached the tree where the girl was standing, she was nowhere to be seen. Paul took out his notebook and drew a rough plan. There were some interesting things to put in. The clearing right in the middle. The fallen tree. A hollow tree-trunk they could creep inside. The ditch round the edge with the plank bridge. And the paths winding about.

'Remember to put in the primroses,' said Harriet. 'The ditch is full of them.'

'I shall do the plan on a big sheet of drawing paper tonight,' said Paul. 'I shall do it in pencil first. Then I'll colour it tomorrow.'

Tea was the best meal of the day at the farm. It was rather late, more like supper, but the work of the day was over and no one was in a hurry. There was plenty of time to sample the good things their aunt had baked in her large, black oven. There were scones and currant bread and fruit cake, tarts and pies and bowls of junket. And something cooked to start with, such as sausages or scrambled egg.

'Uncle,' said Paul, when the farmer had pushed back his chair and was lighting his pipe. 'Tell me about the clearing in the middle of the Round Wood. Why is it there? Why is the grass so green?'

'I can only tell you what my father told me, when I was a boy. He said that long ago, two hundred years or so, the Round Wood was part of a thick forest. There was a road through it which travellers used, and in the clearing there was an inn. Travellers could stay there for the night.'

'Where is it now?' asked Harriet.

'It was burned down long ago. That's why the grass is so green, so some people say. The wood ash fertilised the ground.'

'And a very good thing it *was* burned down,' said their aunt. 'It was an evil place.'

'Evil. Why? How? Do tell us.' The children could not wait to hear.

'It's said – but it may be only a story someone made up – that the innkeeper and his wife were wicked people. They used their young daughter to lure lonely travellers into the inn, and when they were asleep, they killed them and stole their money. There were no banks in those days and travellers often carried large sums of money on them.'

55

'Why didn't the police find out and arrest them?' asked Paul.

'I don't suppose there were any police then. This was a lonely part of the country, as it is today, and no one knew what went on. But they got their deserts. It's said they were burned to death in the fire. But nothing is known for certain.'

'Tell me some more, do, please!' begged Paul.

'I don't know any more to tell.'

'Please try to remember,' added Harriet. 'Had the inn got a name like hotels have today?'

'I've heard it was called *Sleep Well*.'

Paul did his plan in pencil that evening. He left a clear space in the middle and then, as an afterthought, he put in what he imagined was an old inn. He drew it rather like a large, thatched cottage. He enjoyed writing THE ROUND WOOD in capitals and looked forward to colouring them in the next day.

He laid the plan on the top of his chest of drawers in his bedroom, to keep it safe.

Harriet and he talked about the *Sleep Well* inn in bed, wondering how the innkeeper's daughter lured the travellers to their death.

'I expect if she saw a traveller, and if it was getting towards evening, she said: "Clean, cheap beds at the inn, sir. And good food." Or something like that,' suggested Paul.

'But do you think she knew what was going to happen?'

'I don't suppose they'd tell a child. But I expect she guessed.'

'Poor little girl. I'm sorry for her.'

'So am I. I'd hate to have a robber for a father.'

'And for a mother.'

'And worse than robbers. Murderers.'

Harriet felt sure she would have horrid dreams and Paul, feeling that he might, too, said she could come into his bed if she woke and was frightened.

This was a comforting thought and soon both children were asleep.

Next morning, directly he woke, Paul got out of bed to look at his plan. He remembered that he hadn't marked a mossy boulder near the beginning of the path, which they had scrambled on. As he looked at the plan, he gave a cry of surprise.

'Harriet! Wake up! Look at this!'

Harriet yawned and rubbed her eyes, and came to his side.

'Seems O.K. to me,' she said drowsily.

'Look at the inn. I never drew that.'

His thatched cottage had disappeared and in its place, drawn in faded brownish ink, was a kind of roomy log cabin. There was a face at one of the windows, dark and bearded, peering between the curtains. A sign hung over the door and they could just make out the words: SLEEP WELL.

Paul felt sure that neither his uncle nor his aunt would have touched the plan, but he plucked up courage to ask, at breakfast, if anyone had added anything to it during the night.

'Of course not,' said his uncle, indignantly, and Paul knew better than to press the question.

'One bit looked different this morning,' he said. 'I can't remember putting it in last night.'

'Your head was so full of mysteries and murders when you went to bed, I'm not surprised you forgot what you drew,' said his aunt comfortably.

After this, the children got into the habit of playing in the Round Wood when there was nothing else to do, though they helped their uncle on the farm when he would let them, and spent hours with the kitten, Polly, and the farm dog, Rip.

They often took Rip with them to the wood, but he was

57

never happy in the clearing. He whined and shivered and the hair on his spine bristled. They sometimes saw the strange girl but they never got close enough to talk to her. She faded away without a sound. Not a leaf rustled or a twig crackled as she moved out of sight.

On days when they saw her, Rip was specially uneasy and pressed against their legs and looked up at their faces. Once out of the wood, he recovered in an instant, and wagged his tail and sniffed the ground, bolting off after imaginary rabbits and fetching sticks if they were thrown for him.

They asked their uncle if the Round Wood was private.

'Well, it is and it isn't. It's on my land and I could put up a notice saying keep out, but hardly anyone goes there, just hikers in the summer. No one's ever done any damage beyond leaving a few sweet papers about. You see it doesn't lead anywhere.'

'We often see a girl there,' said Harriet boldly. 'But she doesn't want to see us. She disappears.'

They seemed usually to see the girl near a certain tree at the edge of the clearing. One day they had a careful look at the tree, to see if it were in any way special.

'It's very very old,' said Paul, picking at the lichen which had grown over the bark. 'And very twisty.'

'This is rather odd,' said Harriet. 'Just look at this!'

There, among the roots, was a rough cross outlined in pebbles.

'She made it, I'm sure,' said Paul. 'She must have fished the pebbles out of the stream.'

'What do you think it means?'

'I can't guess. In books a cross sometimes means that there's a treasure buried below. We must dig.'

'Dig with what?'

'We'll ask uncle for something.'

During dinner, Paul said: 'Uncle, may we have something to dig with?'

'So you're going to do some gardening? That's a good lad. The place is in a shocking state.'

'No, not exactly. But of course we will help you in the garden another day, if you want us to. We want to dig at the roots of a tree. It's a kind of game.'

Their uncle showed them where the tools were kept and they chose a strong, pointed trowel. Their uncle did not appear at all curious as to why they wanted it.

'Give me a share if you strike gold,' he said with a laugh, as he went off with Rip at his heels.

They dug in turn and found it very hard work. They were on the point of giving up, when Paul heard the trowel ring against something made of metal. Soon they recovered the object which was a metal box. It was surprisingly heavy considering its size.

'It'll be locked, for sure!' wailed Harriet.

But though the hinges were stiff, they managed to prise open the lid.

The spring sunshine came through the trees and shone on the contents. There was a pink necklace made of spiky coral. A small gold cross on a gold chain. A brooch like a daisy, set with tiny pearls, and a child's ring. Harriet slipped this on her middle finger and admired the deep blue stone.

'Look here – look what's at the bottom, all folded up to fit the box exactly.' Paul took out a sheet of paper, opened it and smoothed out the creases. There, carefully painted, was a picture of the inn with the sign outside saying: SLEEP WELL. There was a plume of smoke coming out of the chimney, and a child's swing near the door.

'She could paint better than us,' said Harriet admiringly. 'Look at the sky and the trees and the rough track running by. I suppose that was the road the travellers came along.'

'She's signed it in tiny writing in the corner.'

'Read it to me. It's too tiny. Is the first letter a loopy kind of "E"?'

'I think it says Esther.'

'Poor Esther. These must have been her most precious belongings. I wonder why she hid them.'

'There's something else, underneath, at the very bottom. A kind of little book.' Paul tried, gently, to lift up a corner. 'It isn't a bought one,' he said, as he lifted it out. 'She made it by folding sheets of paper and stitching them together through the middle.'

'What's written on the cover?'

'*MY DIARY written by Esther Fallows.*'

'Let's try to read it, Paul. Please try.'

'The writing is in such pale ink that it may be difficult.'

'Read it out loud to me. I won't interrupt. I expect the ink faded because it's so old.'

Stumbling and hesitating, with many pauses while he puzzled out the words, Paul read it aloud.

Monday 17th. They made me do it again today, though I cried.

Wednesday 19th. I hid in the wood and didn't come home till it was dark. Father beat me.

Sunday 23rd. They made me do it again. Such a nice, kind man. He gave me a groat.

Saturday 29th. A happy day. No one came.

Sunday 30th. Another happy day. No one.

Monday 1st. Happy all day. Wish I could be happy for ever and ever and ever.

Tuesday 2nd. I had to do it again. I cried and said I'd run away. Father said he'd soon catch me and then I'd suffer for it.

Friday 12th. I've decided what I must do. I shall burn the inn down with them inside. There's no other way.

Monday 15th. I've had to do it twice. The first time I sent the man away and said we had no room. But father got to know and he beat me.

Thursday 18th. I shall end it tonight. I've got everything ready. I've buried my treasure box with my dearest possessions in it under the oak. I've prayed for help. I must do it. I must.

When Paul finished reading there was a long silence. Then Harriet said:

'Poor, poor Esther. How brave she was! She ought to be in my book of heroines with Joan of Arc and Grace Darling. She was wonderful. What do you think she meant when she said that she'd got everything ready?'

'I expect she'd put dry sticks about. I don't think they had paraffin in those days. But if it was dry weather the logs the house was built with would burn well. I suppose she was burned too.'

'I don't see why she couldn't have escaped,' said Harriet. 'I would have done.'

'We'll ask uncle and auntie at teatime. But they don't seem to know much.'

'Or care.'

During tea, Paul said to his uncle: 'When the *Sleep Well* inn was burned down, was the innkeeper's daughter burned too?'

'I can't tell you for sure. I suppose so. It was long ago and nothing was written down at the time.'

'We don't know anything,' said his aunt, who did not want the children to be upset. She was a plump, rosy, smiling woman who wanted them all to be comfortable together.

Paul and Harriet decided to keep the jewellery and put the other things back in the box, and to put the box at the foot of the oak again, with a note inside. Paul wrote, in his best hand-writing:

I hope you did not mind us reading your diary. We have kept the jewelry and Harriet says she'll take care of it and give it to her children when she has any. We think

you are very brave. We'll pray for you so that you can rest in peace.

Paul and Harriet

'Why did you say we'd pray for her, Paul? We don't usually pray for people.'

'I've heard that ghosts rest better if someone prays for them. Anyhow, it won't do any harm.'

Harriet picked a few primroses and put them in the box with the letter; five primroses and two leaves, tied round with a blade of grass.

They buried the box lightly so that Esther could dig it up without a trowel. They thought they saw her once among the bushes, but they couldn't be certain. She disappeared, as always, swiftly and silently.

The next day when they came to the wood the box was empty. The letter and the primroses had gone.

A few days later the children left the farm and went home. Before they left, they found a robin's nest in the barn as Harriet had hoped. Paul was praised at school for his map of the Round Wood which he had coloured with Harriet's crayons. Harriet put her map up in her bedroom.

Sometimes, when their mother kissed them good night, she said: 'Sleep well!' She never knew these two words filled them with grief and horror.

The Secret Place

I'm Robert, the middle one. I've an older sister and a younger brother. We live on a farm six miles from a town. It is called High Hill Farm. Everyone says: 'How lovely to live on a farm! What lucky children you are!' Perhaps they are right, but I sometimes wonder. I often think I'd prefer a town with a cinema and shops and a theatre. I want to make films when I grow up, but I never see any except on television and the best ones are often when I've gone to bed. If I lived in a town I could go into the country at weekends, but somehow we only go to town about once in the holidays. Father is too busy to take us. Farmers always are too busy.

I hate being a bus child and having to be by the farm gate at five to eight every morning, to catch the school bus. And I have to come straight home on the bus, too, or mother gets worried and rings up the school. I hate the way the teacher says: 'Line up, bus children.' The village children never have to line up. They can dawdle as much as they like.

The best thing about a farm is the space. Indoors we have large attics where we can play and do what we like. And outside there's the barn and the byre and the stables. Some of the kids at school haven't even room for a kitten. When one of the farm cats has kittens lots of kids want one but their mothers say there isn't room. Not room for a kitten! Then there isn't room for a child, either, I should think.

We have two indoor cats and Meg the dog, and outside

63

there are about ten more cats and more animals than we can count, if you reckon the sheep and the beasts.

Our best playing place is in the tithe barn. It's made of stone and hundreds of years old. It's where the parson stored all the crops the farmers had to give him which was one tenth of everything. It has lovely old stone steps on the outside, rough and uneven but mighty strong. At the other end of the barn there's a curious little room built in the thickness of the wall, no bigger than a big cupboard. No one rightly knows what it was for. We children always call it The Secret Place. Or sometimes S.P. for short.

One day last summer, something very strange happened to me in The Secret Place. I wanted to be alone for a bit, I forget why. Probably because I wanted to write a poem because I may be a poet as well as a film director. Anyhow, The Secret Place is usually pretty quiet, so I went off there. Going up the winding stairs was just as usual, but when I opened the door and went in, it felt different. It sounded different too. There was a whirring, beating sound. It wasn't like a machine, it was more like something alive trying to get out. I felt wings lightly brushing my hair and face and my clothes. I thought it might be a bat, perhaps a whole host of bats, all flapping and flying. But I knew bats were quiet creatures. I know a poem which says: 'Silently flits the bat.' And anyway I've seen bats dozens of times in the evening. My sister used to be afraid one would fly in at her window while she was asleep, and get tangled in her hair. Daddy only said: 'Plait it, then.' But mother said it was an old wives' tale about bats getting caught in human hair. Just nonsense.

Anyhow, I couldn't see a bat or anything else. I kept turning round quickly in case something was lurking behind me. It was a horrid feeling – all those beating wings flicking me and not a thing in sight. Suddenly there was a horrible scream – right in my ear – I didn't wait for anything else to happen,

I scrambled and slipped down the winding stair, grazing my knees and my hands, and ran into the house. It was wonderful to hear a voice on the transistor talking about the weather, and to see my mother making the tea in the fat, round teapot.

'You look a bit upset,' she said calmly. 'And your knee is bleeding.'

'I – I slipped down the steps in the barn,' I said. 'I was startled by something – I think it was a bat.' But I knew it wasn't, really. Only I felt I had to say something. Mother is so used to us children grazing our knees that she didn't fuss. I felt better when I'd drunk my tea. I was shivering before, though it was a warm afternoon.

I didn't tell anyone about my horrid experience in The Secret Place. My brother might have been scared because he is only seven. And my sister would have wanted to tell my father and mother and then everyone would have been talking and discussing and arguing. I felt sure that daddy wouldn't have believed me. He'd have said it was the wind blowing my hair. (He can't bear me wearing my hair long.) Or else that I'd read too many horror comics. (He doesn't approve of comics either.) He's rather a disapproving man, on the whole. But he's going to let me drive one of his tractors next year, which is decent of him.

It was days and days before I dared go to The Secret Place again. I don't think anyone else went there either. Grown-ups never went and we children weren't playing anything special there, just then. Sometimes we pretended it was the hiding place of a wanted man and we took him food and water and kept a look out for enemies.

I waited till I felt really staunch and cheerful. I'd had a good day at school and the tortoiseshell cat had had five kittens. I always feel cheerful when there's a family of kittens around, and I was the only person who knew where these were.

I went up the stone stairs very slowly, this time, and pushed open the door inch by inch. I was listening all the time, but it was dead quiet except for the slight squeak of the hinges. Then I stepped into the room and had nearly as big a fright as I had had before. It wasn't invisible wings beating. It was a visible boy standing in the sunlight.

'Hullo, Robert,' he said.

I couldn't say a word. I was too surprised – and frightened – to speak. I knew at once he was a ghost because I could sort of see through him. I could see the stones of the wall through his clothes. But his clothes looked real enough. And his voice was like a real voice. I thought ghosts gibbered and squeaked, but this one had a cool, thin voice.

I didn't notice his clothes at the time but afterwards I found I could remember them. He had pointed shoes and red stockings with bits of ribbon tied round for garters. He had very peculiar shorts, very full with bits of another colour showing through. They were red and green. He had a sort of dark waistcoat and a shirt with frills of lace round the neck and the wrists. On his left hand he wore a leather glove.

He was a little bigger than me and stood very straight, like as if he was standing at attention. He had a nice face, but sad. I think he had been crying because he rubbed his eyes with the back of his hand.

'I was sorry to give you such a shock the other day,' he said, 'but I couldn't help it. I've come back today to explain. You couldn't see my goshawk, Arrow, though she was flapping and fretting like a mad thing.'

'Why couldn't I see her?' I asked.

'She was terrified of you and ghosts can't become visible if they're terrified. You and I couldn't talk together like this if either was afraid of the other. But we're not, are we, Robert?'

'No,' I said rather doubtfully. 'We're not.'

'It was all so sad – so desperate – that I can't get over it. Neither can Arrow. It was all my fault, and yet I couldn't help it, could I?'

'Can you tell me a little more?' I asked.

The boy smiled slightly. 'Of course. You don't know to what I am referring. It all happened such ages ago, long before

you were born. You see, my father loved the sport of falconry and I loved it too. I learned the art from our master of falconry, one Piers Turbot. I learned so well that I felt sure I could catch a hawk as a mere nestling and feed her and train her and tend her all by myself. I kept my plan secret, though Master Turbot guessed what I was about when he found me trapping rabbits and suchlike for her food. I kept her, hooded, mewed in this small chamber and I spent every spare minute of the day with her. Often I stole out at night and spent some of my sleeping hours with her too. She never slept. Her yellow, ringed eyes, bright as stars, gazed at the world with hatred and scorn. Yet in the end I would have tamed her, I know I would. Already she came quickly to the lure, I swear I would have tamed her by the holy rood.

'I loved Arrow more than I loved anything on earth, more than I loved my parents. The sound of her bewets ringing was the sweetest music I knew. My happiness was complete when I felt her pull on her jesses. I meant to give her silken jesses, not common leather, when I was older.

'Then, when I was out riding with my father, my horse threw me and I fell on my head and suffered a grievous hurt. I knew nothing, not even when they bore me to my bed chamber and laid me on my bed. For nigh a week I lay thus, with my sweet mother weeping at my side and the doctor coming oft to see me. When I came from my swoon, I sat up instantly and tried to stand, crying Arrow – my beautiful Arrow. But I fell back and again knew nought.

'When I woke again, in my right mind, I begged my father to seek my treasure where I had hidden her. He found her dead, hooded and broken. She had starved to death.

'I had other hawks later, swift on the wing and deadly on the kill, but never one that was dear to my heart as Arrow. She was my first love.'

'But why are you here with me now?' I asked.

'When I was still young, a stripling, I died of a fever. Sometimes, the longing for Arrow is so strong that I leave the place of my abode and travel to this narrow, stone room, and here, at times, I am permitted to be with her. She, a wild thing, born free, cannot leave the scene of her birth and captivity and, in the end, her death. She was bewildered when you first heard her wings because she expected me, her

master, and found you, a stranger. She is at peace now. Look well, you will never see her like again.'

Then I saw that on his gloved hand was perched a magnificent hawk. I who knew nothing of falcons and had only seen a hawk as a speck in the sky, soon to fall on its prey like a stone, was breathless. Such beauty! Such power! Such glory! They gazed at each other, boy and bird, then faded slowly till they merged with the grey stone.

Since then, I hardly ever go to The Secret Place. I remember exactly what happened there, what I saw and what I heard. I shall never forget. Never.

When I'm a man and making films of my own, I shall

make one of the boy and his goshawk, Arrow. Do you think it will be too sad? Will no one pay to see it? But I don't know how I can make it different. There can't be a happy ending. There wasn't a happy ending. There never will be, world without end.

Lollipop

'Are you ready yet?' said Guy, tying his tie in front of the mirror. He had only learned to tie it a week ago and it was still a novelty. Soon it would become a bore, like brushing his hair and cleaning his teeth.

'Yes,' said his sister Sue, fastening a last sandal buckle. 'But Lollipop isn't half ready. He just wouldn't get up this morning.'

'I'm tired,' said a high, squeaky voice. 'I didn't sleep a wink. I was counting the stars.'

'You couldn't do that,' said Guy sternly. 'There are far too many.'

'But I did – I did – I did!' said the squeaky voice.

'Then how many were there?'

'A trillion and seven.'

'I just don't believe you,' said Guy.

'Well, it's true, true, true.'

'He's very good at counting,' said Sue kindly. 'Very good indeed.'

'Children, hurry up, do!' their mother called upstairs. 'Your porridge is getting cold.'

'It was all Lollipop's fault,' said Guy. 'He wouldn't get up.'

'He said he was counting the stars all night,' said Sue, 'but he sometimes tells stories.'

'I don't!' said the squeaky voice. 'Or if I do, you tell worse ones.'

'Lollipop!' said Sue. 'Don't answer back or I shall put you outside in the hall.'

'Then I'll scratch the paint with my wee pen-knife.' The voice was louder and squeakier than ever.

The children's father put down his newspaper and spoke firmly:

'No more of this nonsense. Mother and I were talking about you and your silly game last night and we both decided that it must stop. And stop now. No more make-believe people. You've been imagining this horrible creature Lollipop for weeks – for months – and we're sick and tired of him. It's the ghastly squeaky voice we can't stand. You're too old for this silly make-believe, or else we are. Anyhow, it's got to stop.'

'Lollipop will be dreadfully hurt,' said Sue.

'Yes, I am,' said the squeaky voice.

Their father threw the newspaper on the floor and pushed away his plate.

'Can't a man even have his breakfast in peace in his own home? Lollipop must go – vanish – skedaddle. I never want to hear his voice again, and I mean it.'

'But if he won't go?' said Guy.

'Then keep him in your bedroom under lock and key. Better still, send him back to wherever he came from.'

'You're too old for such babyish games,' said their mother gently. 'You'll out-grow him one day, and daddy and I think it should be now. I confess that I can't stand that high-pitched voice myself. And he's dreadfully badly behaved.'

The children exchanged panic-stricken glances. This was the end and they knew it. They ate their breakfast quietly and never said another word, but both found the food difficult to swallow.

'How did Lollipop begin? I've forgotten,' said Sue, as they walked to school, kicking the fallen leaves as they went.

'It was so long ago that I'm not sure,' said Guy. 'I think

I was cross and wouldn't play with you and you said you'd play with Lollipop instead.'

'And you asked me what he was like, and I described him,' said Sue.

'And I added bits.'

'And so did I.'

'And then we got to know him really well,' said Guy. 'What he looked like. What he wore. What he did. Every single thing about him.'

'And now he's our best friend,' said Sue sadly.

'You mean was. He'll never be the same again. We can't just keep him in our bedrooms, all cooped up.'

'He likes to be as free as air,' said Sue. 'Do you remember when he went to the moon in a rocket?'

'Of course I do. And he brought us back some moon-dust.'

'And mother was annoyed because we spilt it on the carpet. She thought it was her powder we'd been messing with.'

'Grown-ups don't know everything.'

'Must we *really* give him up, Guy?'

'We'll have to. I suppose we'll get used to it.'

'I suppose we shall,' sighed Sue.

'But we'll never forget him. Never.'

'Perhaps he'll come back and play with our children when we have some.'

'Perhaps.'

School kept them busy and the children didn't really miss Lollipop till they got home. There was no sound of his squeaky voice while they had tea, though he used to be talkative at tea-time, relating all the naughty things he had done at *his* school, where they had a trampoline and a skating rink and many other delightful features.

'What's on telly?' said Sue.

Guy looked at the *Radio Times*.

'*Sally in our Alley* has just begun.'

73

'I like that because of the animals she keeps. Switch on.'

Guy switched on. There was a series of brilliant round shapes, like balloons, drifting across the screen.

'It's the wrong programme. Try again.'

'No it isn't,' said Guy. 'Let's wait.'

This time, there were slanting lines of tinsel. These changed to puffs of smoke which quickly cleared, and the screen went blank. Soon the picture of a room appeared, with furniture and two children, a boy and a girl watching a television set. Something about the girl's red jersey and blue jeans, and her red hair-band, reminded Sue of somebody.

'Guy, look. That girl is like me, even with my red hairband.'

'And the boy is like me. He's wearing my badge.'

'It is me, and it's you, too,' said Sue.

'But how can it be?' Guy sounded puzzled.

'Let's watch and see what happens.'

Suddenly the picture of the room faded away, and a very strange creature appeared. His hair was like thick, close, black fur and he had round green eyes, like a cat. He was wearing a striped jersey and jeans, and had very long, thin arms.

'Hullo, Guy and Sue,' he said, in a very high sqeaky voice. 'Nice to see you. Now I'll tell you what I've been doing today. Are you sitting comfortably?'

'Yes,' the children whispered.

'Then I'll begin. This morning the first lesson was trampoline and the second lesson was roller skating. The third lesson was history. We're not all that keen on studying history and learning about people who died hundreds of years ago, so three of us went to the school hall and climbed on each other's shoulders and the top one, that was me, put the hands of the big clock forward twenty minutes. When the lesson was half over we began looking at our watches and packing

up our books. Mr Jacobs got very annoyed and in the end he stamped out to look at the hall clock himself. He went off in a huff when he found his own watch was wrong, and forgot to set us any prep, which was a good thing.'

While Lollipop was describing the scene at school, pictures of the school and the children came on the screen, like a film. Guy and Sue laughed and rolled about on their chairs, it was so funny.

'Mother is right,' said Guy, when he could speak. 'Lollipop is certainly badly behaved. I wish we went to that school.'

'So do I,' said Sue. 'I once asked him its name and he said *The School for Silly-billies*.'

Just then their mother came into the room and at once, without a flicker, the programme changed to *Sally in our Alley*.

The children went quietly to bed, but they were seething with excitement.

'It must be magic,' said Sue firmly.

'But I can't see how T.V. came into it,' said Guy. 'We know it was just for us because we are the only ones who know about Lollipop. If only you had seen it, no one would have believed you. I wouldn't have believed you myself.'

'Oh, wouldn't you?' said Sue indignantly. 'I would if it had been only you.'

'No, I wouldn't,' repeated Guy, 'but as both of us saw it we must believe ourselves.'

'It must be magic,' said Sue again. 'And magic can't be explained. So let's not worry. It's like fairies, and ghosts, and dreams. They're all magic.' She sounded pleased and satisfied.

Guy lay awake a long time, thinking about the strange events of the evening. He wanted to tell his mother, but the fact that Lollipop vanished from the screen in a twinkling when she came into the room, made him hesitate. If his

mother knew. Lollipop might never come back. And he wanted above all to see Lollipop again.

The children raced home from school the next afternoon and gobbled their tea so fast, that their mother protested.

'Don't bolt your food as if you were starving. There's plenty more in the larder. And there's ice-cream in the fridge.'

'May we take our ices into the other room and eat them while we're watching telly?' asked Guy.

'No. Eat them properly at the table. There's no hurry. There's no children's programme for twenty minutes.'

But they simply had to hurry. They didn't even notice what flavour the ice-cream was. When they turned the television on, the right programme came at once. It was something for grown-ups which didn't interest them. Then, when the children's programme should have appeared, they saw the same brilliant balloons drifting across the screen. Then the slanting strings of tinsel. Then puffs of smoke. When these cleared, they saw themselves watching the television set in their own sitting-room, clear as a reflection.

After this, came the moment they were waiting for, when Lollipop appeared with his wide smile.

'Are you sitting comfortably, Guy and Sue?' asked the squeaky voice.

'Yes,' they whispered together.

'Then I'll tell you about my trip to the Land of Ice and Snow. I put on my flying suit and revved up my little red helicopter. It rose directly and we made off to the north, the propellors whizzing round. The landscape below was very monotonous, snow and ice, ice and snow, never a tree or a house. Then, as we were flying low, I spied what I'd been looking for. It was a large igloo, built of snow, covered with holly and mistletoe.

'I came down at once. A lantern hung over the doorway, shining on the clusters of red holly berries and the pale mistletoe. There was a painted sign which read:

SANTA CLAUS ESQUIRE
The Toy Workshop

The children had followed all this in a series of pictures, and they saw several reindeer outside the igloo, scraping away the snow with their hooves and browsing on the moss underneath. Their antlers were fine and branched.

They saw Lollipop knock on the door and heard a friendly voice say: 'Come in.'

There sat Santa Claus himself, in a red coat edged with fur, with a white beard and rosy cheeks. He was carving a wooden horse. Toys were stacked all round him, up to the roof. He had a band of helpers dressed in dark green overalls, with red buttons. Some were sewing. Some were cutting out. Others worked at a bench under a bright light, making watches and trains and steamboats. A musical box was playing carols.

'What can I do for you, Lollipop?' asked Santa Claus. 'I'm afraid you've had a cold journey.'

'I've come to make sure you are real,' said Lollipop. 'There are so many rumours going around that you're just make-up. Moonshine. Poppycock. A fraud, in fact.'

'I never listen to gossip,' said Santa Claus, with a chuckle. 'I'm real enough to those that believe in me. As for the others, they're no concern of mine.'

'How do you know what toys to make?' asked Lollipop. 'Are they different every year?'

'I have ways and means of finding out what children want,' said Santa Claus. 'I have my spies. And I have a large post bag.' He pointed to a desk where a white goose in spectacles was going through piles and piles of letters.

'Mother Goose goes through them first and we decide what to do afterwards. Any problems today, Mother Goose?'

'A little boy named Peter wants a talking parrot. We only have squawking parrots in stock.'

'Put a squawking one near the musical box and leave him there. He'll talk all right after a few weeks of Christmas carols in his ear.'

'And a girl named Rosy wants a baby brother, a real one.'

'Give her a baby doll to be getting on with. Anything else?'

'Another boy, Teddy, wants a lion cub with teeth.'

'Oh dear,' sighed Santa Claus. 'When will they learn sense? It would grow into a full-size lion and probably gobble Teddy up for his supper. Try a stuffed lion and make sure it has a fine mane and a set of good teeth.'

'What's popular this year?' asked Lollipop.

'Much the same as usual. Rather a run on moon-rockets and space-ships and helicopters. The girls want dolls with hair that they can shampoo. Some things have quite gone out of fashion. China dolls, for example. Wooden tops and hoops. But they'll come back in time. Children don't change much. It's grown-ups who change more. Anything I can do for you, Lollipop?'

'Not for me, myself,' said Lollipop. 'But for two friends of mine, Guy and Sue. Guy wants roller skates and Sue wants a weaving set, and they both want a kitten. Must be a black kitten.'

'Make a note, Mother Goose, make a note,' said Santa Claus cheerfully.

Guy and Sue exchanged delighted glances. Then, while they were still in the Land of Ice and Snow, the door opened and their father came in. Lollipop vanished from the screen and a Mickey Mouse cartoon appeared instead.

'Is it a good programme?' asked their father.

'Smashing!' said Guy.

'Fantastic!' said Sue.

He stayed to watch with them and when the programme was finished he expressed amazement that they found such nonsense enjoyable.

'You should have seen what went before,' said Guy. 'You'd have had the surprise of your life.'

Every night, if the children could arrange to be alone when they switched on the television, Lollipop appeared on the screen and they watched his adventures. He never came to any harm and he never hurt anyone else, but he led an exciting life. They never, quite, lost the thrill of seeing themselves in the picture too, at the beginning.

The magic only worked at a certain time. Earlier or later, the programmes stayed as printed in the newspaper.

Lollipop tied the corners of his handkerchief to a toy soldier and dropped him from an upstairs window. The handkerchief filled with air like a parachute. Then he tied the four corners of a tablecloth to himself and jumped off the roof. Sue screamed and shut her eyes, but she need not have been so frightened. Little, feathery wings sprouted from Lollipop's shoulders and he flapped safely down. His life was full of adventures and quite different from theirs, just as his face was quite different with its close fur for hair, and round green eyes, and a wide smile that stretched from ear to ear.

The only thing that spoiled the children's meetings with Lollipop was the fact that they had to be kept secret. At first they enjoyed feeling special, and knowing that a pro-

gramme appeared every evening just for them alone. But they found that a secret kept too long became a burden instead of a joy. They longed above all to share it with someone else.

They decided early on that they should not tell their parents as that would mean the end of Lollipop. Now, they wondered if they could tell another child, as Lollipop seemed to like children. But who?

Guy wanted to tell a boy named Max, who was older and bigger than himself. He wanted Max to look up to him for a change.

Sue, on the other hand, had a close friend named Poppy whom she had had all her life. They even shared the same birthday. She felt that by telling Poppy they would almost be keeping the secret in the family.

After many discussions, Guy suddenly gave in. 'We'll tell Poppy,' he said. 'I think Max might want to tell his friends in the next form and we don't want the secret spread all through the school. Tell Poppy when you like.'

Sue lost no time and told Poppy the whole story at break. Poppy behaved perfectly. She didn't ask too many questions and was very pleased to be told a secret – almost any secret. She did not even ask to *see* the wonderful Lollipop. She just listened with eyes wide open. And marvelled.

'Wouldn't you like to see him for yourself?' prompted Sue.

'Oh, if I could! It would be the most exciting thing that has ever happened to me. But how?'

Guy and Sue had talked about ways and means, so Sue could answer without hesitation:

'We'll ask you to tea. When we turn on the telly we'll hide you behind the sofa. When we give you a signal, you can come out and watch with us.'

'Ask me soon!' begged Poppy. 'Ask me today!'

Sue's mother was not surprised when Sue asked if she

could have Poppy to tea. Poppy was often in and out of the house.

'Why, of course, darling. When would you like to have her?'

'Today, please.'

'I'd rather it was tomorrow,' said her mother, 'then I'll get something nice for tea. Yes, ask her for tomorrow.'

The next day, Poppy came home with them from school and was so excited that she could hardly eat the special tea, though it was sausages and chips and raspberry cream. Afterwards they went into the sitting-room. They had to wait quarter of an hour for their programme and they could not settle to do anything. They piled the cushions on the floor and jumped into them from the sofa, to pass the time.

'You should see Lollipop's trampoline,' said Guy. 'But of course you may not see it tonight. We never know what we're going to see till it happens.'

'He said he might go to the zoo,' said Sue. 'I hope he does. He's sure to do something ridiculous like getting into the monkeys' cage and playing with the monkeys.'

'Or making the lions roar,' suggested Guy.

'I shan't like that,' said Poppy nervously. 'I'm scared of lions.'

'Guy's only guessing,' said Sue comfortingly. 'He may not even go to the zoo. Oh, the clock has just struck. Hide behind the sofa, Poppy.'

Poppy hid and Guy turned on the set. At once the rainbow balloons floated over the screen. Then came the slanting strings of tinsel. Then the smoke. As it cleared, the familiar picture of Guy and Sue in front of a television set appeared.

Lollipop landed in the middle of the screen with a jump.

'Hullo, everybody,' he said in his squeaky voice, smiling his ear-to-ear smile. 'Today I've been decorating the Christmas tree. Are you sitting comfortably? Then I'll tell you about it.'

'Come out,' whispered Guy, leaning over the back of the sofa. Poppy, with cheeks as red as a real poppy, darted out. Then several things happened at once. There was a blinding flash and a loud explosion. Then the screen went dark.

'He's gone,' cried Sue. 'He's gone for ever and he'll never come back!'

'Was it my fault?' asked Poppy, looking panic-stricken. 'I didn't know –'

Then their mother, who had heard the bang, came running in.

'We didn't do anything, mother, honest,' said Guy. 'We were just sitting watching and there was the flash and the bang.'

'Something must have gone – perhaps a valve,' said their mother. 'Daddy will have to look at it when he comes home. We've had no trouble with the set before. It was bound to happen sometime. For heaven's sake don't cry, Sue. It wasn't your fault. It was an accident. Shall we all play ludo to cheer ourselves up?'

Three very silent children joined in the game without the usual yells of rage when they got sent home, or the scream of joy when they threw a six.

After that, they seldom mentioned Lollipop, even when they were alone. At Christmas they were given a tiny black kitten and as Sue stroked his soft black fur she said to Guy:

'His name is Lollipop.'

'Yes,' said Guy. 'It's Lollipop.' The two exchanged glances, remembering Lollipop's furry black hair. Then they forgot him again, playing on the stairs with the new Lollipop.

A Tale of Sorrow

Phoebe and Lucy were staying with their Aunt Jane, who was a housekeeper at a home for old people. The guests, as Aunt Jane called them, had their own rooms and belongings and could walk in the extensive gardens, if they were able, and sit in the summer house, if the sun was shining. Just now it was the Christmas holidays and few of them ever ventured out.

The oldest gentleman there was eighty-nine, and the oldest lady was a hundred. Sometimes the girls talked to the old lady who was wrapped in a pink woolly shawl like a baby, but had a lively pair of bright blue eyes. She sometimes thought they were *her* grandchildren and called them Effie and Alice by mistake.

Phoebe and Lucy had not wanted to go and stay at Oakley Manor, as the Home was called, because they could not imagine what they could possibly do all day. But they knew they must make the best of it, as their mother was taking a course so that she could get a job as a nursery school teacher, and there was no one at home to look after them.

They thought the Home might be rather like a hospital with a queer, stuffy smell and slippery red corridors. But it had proved a lovely place, stone built, with tall chimneys and steps up to the door. They slept and played in a large, disused attic where they could make as much noise as they liked. Aunt Jane had her own television which they could watch when they wanted, and the library van brought books that they could borrow every Thursday. They had both just taken

up knitting; Phoebe was attempting a jersey and Lucy was knitting a long scarf, striped in black and yellow like a wasp.

What with knitting and reading and watching television and chatting to the guests, they weren't bored at all. When the sun shone, they played in the large, neglected garden and had begun to make a den in the shrubbery, a thing they couldn't have done in the tiny back yard at home.

One night, Phoebe tossed and turned in her bed, and shook her pillow. The bed creaked dismally. She felt she would never get to sleep, however hard she tried. All the while she was listening, even when she drew the bed-clothes up over her ears. At last she could bear it no longer, and sat up straight.

'Lucy, I can hear it again.'

'So can I.'

'It's been going on for ages and ages. I've been hiding my head under the blankets, but that's no good.'

'I'll never get to sleep, never,' said Lucy.

'We must *do* something.'

'But what?' answered Lucy wearily. 'We've looked outside before and there was no one there. Aunt Jane says there are no children in the house except us.'

'Oh, listen! It must be a child, it must. And it sounds as if it's just outside the door. I'm going to look again.'

'Wait for me. I'm not going to be left here all alone.'

Phoebe turned on the bedside light and they both put on dressing-gowns and slippers. Then Phoebe opened the door quietly.

It was light on the landing and the stairs, yet everything was different. A gas jet burned dimly on the wall and the dull, purple carpet that flowed all over the house like a purple sea, had disappeared. The stairs were bare boards. Halfway down, a girl in a white nightdress was crouching, sobbing as if her heart would break. Her hair was combed tightly back and plaited in two, knobbly black pigtails.

Phoebe touched her on the shoulder and found she was shaking with the cold, or the sobbing, or both.

'Don't cry. Can we help you?' she said softly.

'You'd cry if your chilblains hurt like mine. I can't bear it! I can't bear it! It's even worse than the workhouse. And I'm so unhappy.' The sobs began again.

Phoebe took one of the child's hands in hers. It was thin, but the fingers were rough and red and swollen. Some had deep raw cracks. A bit of rag was tied round her forefingers.

'Your mother ought to take you to the doctor and he'd give you something to make them better.'

The child looked up with scorn in her black eyes and said sharply:

'Whoever heard of anyone going to a doctor with chilblains? All the children at the workhouse had them. But mine are much worse here. It's all the hard work and my hands in and out of buckets and sinks all day. It stands to reason I get chilblains.'

'Why are your hands in and out of buckets?' asked Lucy curiously.

'Because I'm the scullery maid, of course.'

'You can't be a maid, you're only a child like me.'

'Oh, can't I? That's all you know. When I was twelve, the master at the workhouse got me this place here, at Oakley Manor. He said I was a lucky girl. I don't *feel* a lucky girl, I can tell you.' And the tears began again.

'What do you do all day, do tell us,' asked Phoebe.

The tears gradually subsided.

'Well, I get up at five o'clock and scrub the kitchen and the scullery and do the hall. And when it's light I do the steps in the front. Even if it's freezing cold I have to do them. Then all day long, I never stop. I work under the cook and every moment it's: "Get the potatoes done – scrape the carrots – cut up the onions. Fetch the coal – wash this –

scour that – sweep the hearth." And the cook is that bad tempered. She's handy with the ladle, too!'

'What do you mean: "Handy with the ladle"?' asked Phoebe.

'I mean she hits me with it. I've a lump on my head now the size of an egg. I can't comb my hair. I hate her. She's a foul-mouthed creature. But she can cook. My lady says her soufflés are light as air, and my lord says her syllabubs are a poem.'

'What is your name? Mine is Phoebe and my sister is Lucy.'

'I'm called Sorrow.'

There was a silence. Her hearers did not know what to say. Then Lucy asked gently:

'Why did your mother choose that name?'

'It wasn't my mother. She came into the workhouse one night and I was born in the morning, and my mother died. So the workhouse kept me and brought me up and called me Sorrow.'

'What did they teach you?'

'Mostly plain sewing and how to work. I used to hope they'd let me clean the brass candlesticks in the parlour. That was an interesting job.'

'Didn't you do lessons?'

'I learned a lot of stuff by heart, the collects and the psalms. I say them to myself when I can't get to sleep, but tonight my chilblains hurt too much. My feet are the worst. And the black boots they gave me when I was fitted out for service pinch me something terrible. They're good, strong boots, all the same. I like to polish them, when I have the time.'

'Is your room nice and cosy?' asked Phoebe.

'Cosy? What do you mean?'

'Oh, warm, and a soft, warm bed and lots of blankets. You know – cosy. Comfortable.'

'My room is cold as charity and I've only one blanket, but

I roll myself up in it. And I have a lovely soft pillow. The workhouse pillow was stuffed with straw.'

'Would you like my hot water-bottle?' said Lucy. 'It still feels fairly warm.'

'Hot water-bottle?' Sorrow opened her big black eyes in surprise.

'To warm your bed. Look, I'll fetch it and show you.'

Lucy offered her the bottle which had a pink, fluffy cover.

'For me? For my bed?'

'Yes. Cuddle it and then, perhaps, you'll get to sleep.'

'I've never seen the like before,' marvelled Sorrow. 'When one of the quality is ill we heat up a brick in the oven and wrap it up in flannel and warm their bed with it. But this is so soft – so warm. Are you a lady?'

Lucy looked puzzled. 'No, I'm only a little girl. I suppose I'll grow into one some day.'

'I won't ever,' said Sorrow firmly. 'I'll always be a servant. But one day I might rise to be a nursery maid. Then I could wait on the children and live in the nursery wing. It's lovely there, warm and bright with a rocking horse and a dolls' house and all manner of toys. I sometimes fill the coal-scuttle in there, or take up a tray if the nursery maid is too busy.'

'Don't you ever play?' asked Phoebe.

' 'Course not. What do you take me for? When I left the workhouse the master said to me: "Sorrow, you're not a child any more. You're a woman. Mind you behave like one." '

'We play most of the time,' said Lucy. 'We shan't be women for years and years. I'm eleven and Phoebe is twelve like you.'

'I did once ride on the rocking horse,' confessed Sorrow, 'when the children were away at the seaside. And I looked at the dolls. One had real hair.'

'Haven't you a doll of your own? Or didn't you have one when you were at the workhouse?'

'I had a wax doll once, off the Christmas tree, when I was little, about five. But the master took it off me and burned it when he found I'd taken it to church. Toys weren't allowed in church.'

'Was she beautiful?' inquired Lucy.

'Oh, she was. Golden hair and blue eyes and a real dress and chemise. I loved her. I called her Polly.'

'I would have kicked that horrible master,' said Phoebe fiercely.

'Then you'd have been beaten black and blue and put on bread and water,' said Sorrow calmly, 'and that wouldn't have brought your doll back.'

'You'd better go to bed while the bottle is warm,' said Lucy. 'Good night, Sorrow. Let me put some cold cream on your poor hands before you go. It's the only thing mother gave us. It's for if our noses get sore when we have a cold.'

Lucy fetched the jar and gently rubbed the cream on the red, swollen fingers. Sorrow looked blissfully happy as she felt the soft touch and the softer cream.

'That was real lovely. It's done me a power of good. Good night.'

She went up the last few steps in her bare feet and faded into the shadows. The girls scrambled back into their own beds.

'Mine's not quite cold,' said Phoebe.

'Nor is mine, quite. But very nearly. If I were Sorrow I'd just die of misery.'

'I wouldn't ever die,' said Phoebe, 'but I'd run away.'

Soon they were fast asleep.

The next day was sunny and frosty and they played in the shrubbery all the morning. But they could think of nothing except Sorrow. They found the bottle, stone cold, outside their door when they woke up. They were not sure exactly what a workhouse was, so they asked their Aunt Jane when they next saw her.

'There aren't any workhouses now,' replied their aunt. 'But there were a hundred years ago, perhaps less. They were the only places where people who were old and homeless and and had no money could go. I believe they turned no one away. But they had to work hard cleaning the place to pay for their lodgings.'

'Who looked after the people?'

'A master.'

'Was he always cruel?'

'I really don't know, but I suppose some masters were kind and some were hard.'

'Could children go there?'

'If their parents went they'd take their children with them.'

'And the orphans?'

'The workhouse kept them till they were old enough to get a job. The boys might go on a farm and the girls became servants. I don't know much about them. You're old enough to read Dickens' *Oliver Twist*, Phoebe. You'll learn more then.'

Phoebe decided to ask if there was a copy in the library van when Thursday came round.

The next night there was no sobbing to disturb the girls, but when they had been asleep some time, Phoebe woke and said:

'I think she's there.'

'So do I. I thought I heard a tap on the door.'

'Yes. A kind of scratch.'

'Let's go and see.'

They put on their light and quickly found their dressing-gowns and slippers, and opened the door. There sat Sorrow, on the top step this time, and again the carpet had disappeared and the gas jet spluttered on the wall. They sat down one on each side of her, and tried to keep her warm.

'What have you been doing today?' asked Phoebe.

'Working, same as any other. I had to clean out the

cupboard under the stairs. It was dark and a rat jumped out at me. But it didn't bite.'

'I should hope not! Weren't you scared?'

'I'm more scared of the cook and her ladle. Rats mean no harm. They don't like being disturbed, that's all. The cook put broken glass at the mouth of the hole but I took it away when her back was turned and hid it in the cellar. No rat ever hurt me.'

'We played in the shrubbery and got on with our den,' said Lucy.

'What's that?'

'A play house made of branches and an old sack. We pretend we live there.'

'It's a queer life you lead,' said Sorrow, in a puzzled voice. 'No work and all play. Wait till you're grown-up and have to go out to earn your bread!'

'I'm going to be a concert pianist,' said Phoebe.

'And I shall marry and have twin babies,' said Lucy. 'My husband will earn the bread. The children and I will eat it.'

'Did you have a nice supper, Sorrow?' asked Phoebe.

'When the cook and the upper servants had finished and I had washed up and left the kitchen tidy, the cook let me have a bowl of soup and some bread and dripping. It was very tasty. But I could have eaten a whole loaf, I was that hungry.'

Lucy put some more cold cream on Sorrow's chilblains and lent her her hot-water bottle. Even the girls were shivering in their warm dressing-gowns. Draughts seemed to whistle down from the roof. They said good night to Sorrow as before, and she faded noiselessly into the shadows.

The next night was one they never forgot for the rest of their lives. They woke about eleven and crept out of their room on to the bare stairs. Sorrow was already there, her face dead white and her plaits dark and stiff.

'Will your cream swale this away?' she asked, pushing

back the sleeve of her nightgown. On the back of one wrist was a livid, angry burn.

'It might do some good,' said Phoebe, who had taken her First Aid Badge, 'but it won't cure that awful burn. However did you do it?'

'I didn't do it. Cook did.'

'But how? Not on purpose? What happened?'

'I had to iron her white apron and I was careless and I didn't test the iron and it was too hot. It left a great brown scorch mark right on the front. And it was a new apron. She said she'd learn me to spoil other people's clothes and she pressed the iron on my wrist.'

'The beast! The pig! The wretch!' said Phoebe. 'She's a torturer like the Spanish Inquisition. She could go to prison for ages for that. Perhaps for life!'

'I *did* spoil her best apron,' said Sorrow reasonably. 'I was careless. I was thinking of our lovely talk the night before. And the hot-water bottle. And the cold cream. I wasn't thinking what I was doing. They used to teach us at the workhouse to mind our betters and try to please.'

'She's not your better. She's your worse! She's the worst cook in the world. She ought to be roasted in her own oven like the witch in *Hansel and Gretel*. I'd spit at her if she did that to me!' Phoebe clenched her fists.

'She's kind sometimes,' said Sorrow. 'She lets me play with the kitten when I've done my work and on Sunday she once let me look at the pictures in her bible. It has lovely pictures. The one of Daniel in the lions' den is a treat. And so are the angels going up and down the ladder in Jacob's dream.'

'What's that chain round your neck,' said Lucy, catching a gleam of gold above the neck of Sorrow's nightdress.

'It's my locket and chain. It's the only thing my mother left me. She put it round my neck. The master took it away and kept it safe, but he gave it back to me the day I came to Oakley Hall. I wear it always, day and night. It's my very

own. But you can look at it, if you like. Isn't it pretty? It's real gold.'

Lucy looked at it and passed it to Phoebe, who looked carefully at the pattern chased on it.

'May I open it? It has a hinge.'

'Yes.'

Phoebe opened it and took out a crumpled, much folded, scrap of paper. It had faded writing on it.

'What does it say, Sorrow?'

'I don't know. I never learned to read and write very well, though I can figure a little and I know some tables. Read it to me.'

The ink was pale and the writing strange and loopy, but Phoebe read it out slowly:

'Please take my little daughter to my sister Prue at The Dolphin Tavern, hard by Queenshithe Wharf, London.'

'They ought to have taken you there at once,' said Phoebe. 'Prue would be your proper aunt, like our Aunt Jane. She'd have adopted you and brought you up as hers. It may not be too late now.'

'No one knew about the paper. No one would think it of any consequence.' Sorrow looked stricken. Her dark eyes slowly filled with tears.

'You must run away from this place. Do you know how to get to London?' Phoebe's voice was confident and encouraging, as she closed the locket and put it back round Sorrow's neck.

'That I do. I know well. The coach passes these very gates about the stroke of midnight. Sometimes guests leave by it and I have to keep the parlour fire up and give the gentlemen a cheesecake or summat for the journey. I'll go tonight to my Aunt Prue and be her little girl.'

The tears had vanished and her face was calm and determined.

'Supposing –' Lucy hesitated. 'Supposing she isn't there any longer. Supposing she's moved away, or –'

'Or dead,' put in Sorrow. 'I don't care. I'll take my chance. I'm a strong wench and I can work. I can scrub and scour a fair treat. I'll come to no harm.'

Phoebe and Lucy were thinking the same thoughts, though they both kept quiet. This poor, thin scrawny child was not their idea of a 'strong wench', with wrists no thicker than a baby's. Her legs, below her nightgown, were like sticks with purple, swollen feet. But they knew there was a spirit like steel inside the skin and bone.

'I'll get packed,' said Sorrow. 'I've an old basket I brought my bits and pieces in from the workhouse. My boots are well polished. I'll not be long.'

'Let's see what we can give her,' said Lucy.

'We must be quick,' replied Phoebe. 'We mustn't make her lose the coach. I'm sure we can spare lots of things. Oh, I can't think. I'm too excited to think. I shall die of excitement.'

They rushed round their room snatching up this article and that, and they found Sorrow outside, dressed in her black boots, with a shawl over her shoulder and a funny little poke bonnet. The basket was on the landing at her feet.

'Quick, take this – and this – and let me push this in the corner.' They opened the basket and added some handkerchiefs, some socks, a pair of gloves, two hair-bands and Phoebe's doll, a tiny Japanese lady in a kimono.

'Good-bye, Sorrow. We'll never forget you, never.'

They kissed her warmly and she kissed them back and clung to them, her eyes shining with joy. She sped down the stairs, carrying her basket by the handle, and girls rushed to the staircase window. This had a clear view of the wrought-iron gates. Supposing they were locked at night? What then? But the gates were not locked and they saw

Sorrow slip through, her figure looking smaller than ever in the distance.

They waited, their hearts beating frantically, holding hands tightly, but not speaking. At last they heard the

rumble of the coach and the trample of horses feet. The coach drew up. Sorrow disappeared inside and the coach rolled on into the night. Sorrow had gone, for better or worse. They would never know which.

It was three years later. Phoebe was fifteen and Lucy fourteen. Their mother was teaching in a nursery school of her

own and the girls were proud of her. They all set out together in the morning and shared the household tasks when
they got home, though these did not include washing the
front step.

Phoebe and Lucy remembered every detail of the strange
events at Oakley Hall, where the oldest inhabitant had died
a year ago, aged a hundred and two. They seldom spoke of
Sorrow, partly because there seemed an increasing number
of things to be done. There was school, and their homework,
and their knitting when they remembered it, and Phoebe
had her piano practice to fit in.

Exactly three Christmases after their visit to Aunt Jane,
their father took them to London for a week to see the sights.
It was crisp, frosty, weather and they walked miles through
parks and gardens, museums and picture galleries, visiting
many famous buildings.

Before they came home, they had a spare day to buy
presents and do just what they chose.

'What's your fancy?' asked their father. 'You choose as
long as it isn't Madame Tussaud's again or the whispering
gallery at St Paul's.'

Phoebe and Lucy exchanged glances.

'We'd like to go and see *The Dolphin Tavern*.'

'Why not? We'll have lunch there as a change from these
eternal sandwich bars. Where is it?'

'We don't know. Near Queenshithe, we think. But it may
not exist at all.'

'Why this sudden interest in a place that may not
exist?'

'Oh, it did once. And it isn't a sudden interest. We've
had it for three years. We heard of it when we were staying
with Aunt Jane.'

'A bit of a mystery, is that it? Well, wait while I look up
my map and guide book. And you might fetch the telephone
directory – letter D.'

After leafing through the directory and unfolding the map, their father said with satisfaction:

'Well, it's there all right, in a part of London we haven't visited. We'll take a bus and then walk.'

The girls said little. They did not know what they expected, but they were not disappointed when they reached *The Dolphin Tavern*. It was a stone-built building among a welter of brick buildings, with little iron railings round the windows and a group of tall chimneys. The sign of a blue and silver dolphin hung over the door.

They warmed themselves by an open fire while sipping fruit juice and nibbling crisps. The waiter led them to a table by the window.

Lucy was trying to attract Phoebe's attention. She gestured to a portrait on the wall and whispered:

'There she is. It's Sorrow herself. I'm sure it is.'

Phoebe looked at the portrait which was in oils. It showed a tall, thin lady with dark eyes and jet-black hair, plaited and coiled at the back of her head. She wore a black, striped dress with a high neck and frills of lace at the neck and the cuffs. She wore a gold locket on a slender chain. Their father felt their excitement and looked too.

'Waiter, can you tell us anything about this portrait? It is very striking.'

'Why, I can tell you what I know, which isn't much. The portrait is Mrs Sorrow Garland.'

The girls exchanged delighted glances, as the man went on.

'She owned this place long ago when it became famous. She was a grand cook and the tavern got its reputation for its apple turnovers which were made from some secret recipe that was never divulged. She married the son of the Lord Mayor of London and had a large family, I believe.'

'You see, she became a lady after all,' said Lucy to Phoebe. 'Do you remember, she said whatever happened she'd always stay a servant? I'm so glad she was wrong.'

'I'm sure she was kind to the servants under her,' said Phoebe, 'and never used her ladle except to ladle out soup.'

'I don't know what you're talking about,' said their father, 'but this onion soup is very good. And we'll try the famous apple turnovers afterwards. Start while it's hot.'

The girls took up their spoons and did just that.

The Water Spirit

There was once a little boy named Nigel, who went to stay with his grandmother. She lived a long way off. He had never seen her before, though she often sent letters and presents. He felt sure he would like her because she was so kind, but he was not sure that he would like being so far from home.

His grandmother lived in an old stone house with a large, wild garden all round. An old gardener tried to keep the paths clear, and to stop the shrubs and bushes from covering the windows so no one inside could look out. But that was about all he could manage.

The lawns were like hay fields, and the rambler roses and other climbing plants scrambled everywhere.

Nigel thought it was the best garden he had ever seen; not like the parks in the town where he lived with never a weed, and the flowers in tidy rows or neat beds.

Nigel was used to racing about with a gang of friends, and here he had to play by himself, but he did not mind. Sometimes, when he was passing a tree, it spoke to him, and said in a deep voice:

'Climb me! Climb me!'

If Nigel tried, he always found it was a very good tree for climbing, with branches well placed for his feet, and handholds just where he needed them.

Other trees said:

'Do not climb me! Do not climb me!' and if Nigel disobeyed and tried, he always found there were nettles or

prickly bushes at the bottom, and the branches were too far apart, or so rotten that they broke easily.

So he soon learned to trust the trees. As he was very fond of climbing, and there were no trees near his home to climb, he spent hours playing on the trees in the garden. He often got almost to the top and had a lovely view. He felt nearly as high as the tall chimneys of the house.

It was a hot summer, and Nigel was pleased when he found a little stream. He wasn't sure if it belonged to his grandmother or not, but he never saw anyone else about, so he played by it quite happily.

In one place the stream became wider and there was a deep, green pool under a drooping willow. It was so clear that he could see the stones and waterweed at the bottom. He often paddled in it and the water was strangely warm. He could play in it all the afternoon and not feel cold.

One day, when he was making a wall of stones across the stream, the rippling water spoke to him. It had a clear, high voice, not at all like the husky whisper of the trees.

'Bathe in me! Bathe in me!' said the stream.

'Why not?' thought Nigel, and he took off his clothes and slowly lowered himself into the water. It still felt warm, even on his back and his shoulders.

The pool was never deeper than just above his waist, so he felt safe. He could almost swim because he went to the baths with his form at school, but he hadn't quite got the knack.

Here, in this calm water, with no one splashing him or pushing him, he learned to swim four strokes. He might have managed more, six or seven or ten, but there was only room to do four, and then the water got too shallow. They were four breast strokes because he had not learned any other strokes yet.

He found he could float, too, and he often lay on his back in the water, floating, and looking up through the branches

of the willow. Arrows of sunlight came through the branches, and where they fell on the water it sparkled.

So Nigel began to visit the pool every day, and every day the water said in a friendly voice:

'Bathe in me! Bathe in me!'

Nigel was out of his clothes in a flash, and swimming in the warm pool, or floating under the willow, or just playing about. He sailed sticks for boats, and dropped stones, which fell down, down to the bottom, stirring the mud a little. They left rings on the surface of the water which spread and spread till they could spread no more.

One hot morning, Nigel woke up early and his first thought was the pool. After breakfast he went upstairs to his grandmother's room to say good morning to her. She always had her breakfast in bed, on a silver tray.

'Good morning, granny.'

'Good morning, Nigel. Are you happy here?'

'Very happy, granny.'

'Are you lonely?'

'Not at all, granny.'

'What do you do all day long?'

'I play.'

'What do you play at?'

'I climb trees, and I –' he paused.

'And what, Nigel? You can tell me anything. I am never angry.'

'And I bathe in the pool in the stream, under the willow.'

'Just like your father!' said his grandmother. 'They were the things he liked doing best, climbing and swimming, when he was your age. Now kiss me, child, and go off and be happy.'

Nigel kissed her cheek, and ran away down the path that led to the stream. As he brushed past the trees, he heard some of them murmur:

'Climb me! Climb me!' but he didn't stop to listen.

When he got to the pool, he began to unbuckle his sandals, when he noticed there was something different. Something wrong. The water was speaking to him in its high, clear voice, but it was saying:

'Do not bathe in me! Do not bathe in me!'

'Why ever not?' asked Nigel.

But the water just repeated, over and over:

'Do not bathe in me! Do not bathe in me!'

Everything looked as usual, except that the water was not quite as clear. There had been rain in the night, and Nigel thought there might be more water running by, and that the mud at the bottom might have been churned up.

'All right,' he said. 'I'll come back later.'

He climbed his favourite tree, an oak, and played with his bow and arrow, then ran back to the pool. The water still said:

'Do not bathe in me! Do not bathe in me!'

Nigel walked slowly away, and helped the gardener who was cutting back some bushes. He picked up the clippings and piled them in the wheelbarrow for the old man.

During the afternoon he visited the pool half a dozen times, but the water was always saying the same thing. He went there just before bedtime to see if the words had changed, but he was not really surprised to hear the now familiar:

'Do not bathe in me!'

The next day was scorching hot. He just wore shorts and sandals as the thinnest shirt was too much.

'You could fry an egg on these stone steps,' said the gardener, who was sweeping them. The stone almost burned Nigel's hand when he touched it.

Down to the pool he hurried, only to hear once again the warning:

'Do not bathe in me.'

'But why not?' said Nigel. 'Why ever not? If you can

talk, just tell me why not! The pool isn't deeper. The current isn't stronger. What's different from usual? Tell me! Only tell me!'

He found himself shouting though the voice of the water stayed gentle and quiet.

'Why not? Why not?' he said again.

He took off one sandal and dipped his toes into the water. Then, very slowly, his whole foot. Then he took off his other sandal so that both feet were in together. He lowered them till the water was over his ankles – halfway up his calves – then right up to his knees. It felt cool and silky. The voice was now silent, and he began to whistle to fill the silence.

'There's nothing wrong!' he said out aloud. 'And it's just the day for a bathe.'

'Yes, so it is,' said a new, harsh voice, and he felt himself seized in two, long, green arms, and pulled down – down – down.

Nigel did not splutter or choke as he found he could breathe quite easily in the dim, under-water world where the arms had dragged him. He saw that the person holding him was green all over, and covered with scales like a fish. His eyes were emerald and gave out beams of light like head-lights.

'Who are you?' he asked.

'I am the Water Spirit. The pool and all that is in it is mine. And now that you have ventured into the pool you are mine too.'

'I'm not. I belong to myself. Let me go at once!' and Nigel struggled and tried to bite the slippery green hands that held him. 'Let me go!'

'I shall never let you go,' said the Water Spirit. 'Never! Never! Never! You are mine!'

'Unless he guesses your magic riddle,' said a little voice from above. It was a wagtail, perched on the willow. Nigel

could see that the wagtail had made the Water Spirit angry.

'If you guess the magic riddle you'll break the spell,' went on the wagtail. 'I'm right, aren't I?'

'Yes,' said the Water Spirit crossly. 'But he won't guess it. He isn't clever enough.'

'At least I can try,' said Nigel. 'Ask me.'

'Yes, just ask him,' said the wagtail.

'This is the riddle,' said the Water Spirit.

*Bury my heart
In an earthy bed,
A giant will spring up
With leaves round his head,
And on every finger
A ruby red.*

'I'll give you time to think,' said the Water Spirit. 'I'll give you till the sun is just over that tall poplar.'

'Can I think on dry land? I feel rather queer and stuffy down here.'

'Yes, you may sit on the bank. But remember, I shall snatch you back if you move an inch.'

So Nigel sat on the bank and thought. The wagtail flew away among the trees.

'*an earthy bed* – that must be the soil, perhaps a hole dug in it. *A giant with leaves on his head* – that might be someone very tall with a hat of leaves. *And on every finger a ruby red* – he must be someone rich to be wearing all those rings. *On every finger* – that sounds silly. I wonder if it means thumbs as well.'

The more he thought, the more muddled he became. Every time he looked at the sun it was a little nearer to the top of the poplar. He must think of something soon.

Just then the wagtail flew back, fluttering her wings, and chirping. She laid something by Nigel's hand and he quickly picked it up.

What could it be? Round and small and hard. Too small for a plum stone. Too big for a grape pip, or an apple pip. Could it be an orange pip, or even a lemon pip? But it wasn't the right shape, and not pale enough. He was sure he had seen things like it before. But where? Why, of course, it was a cherry stone. That was the answer. Plant it and a tree would grow up, bearing leaves and red cherries. That was the answer.

'The answer is a cherry!' he shouted. 'A cherry!'

The change in the Water Spirit was horrible to watch. He grew smaller and thinner and a paler green, till he was like a ghost.

'My power has passed!' he wailed. 'I'm weak as water weed! I'm feeble as a frog! I'm powerless as a paper boat!'

With a shriek and a shudder, he vanished into the pool. Soon the ripples ceased spreading...

When Nigel said goodbye to his grandmother before leaving for home, she said to him:

'Well, you soon got tired of bathing in the pool. Your father was just the same as a boy, he had crazes for things. Sometimes it was climbing – then bathing – then making dens – always something new.'

'But I *did* learn to swim,' said Nigel, 'and I'll never forget how. Once you learn to swim you remember all your life. And there are other things, too, that I shall remember all my life,' he added to himself.

As the train sped on its way towards home and the town and his friends, the sound of the wheels seemed to fit in with something running through his head:

> *Bury my heart*
> *In an earthy bed,*
> *A giant will spring up*
> *With leaves round his head,*
> *And on every finger*
> *A ruby red.*

Not Waving—But Drowning

There's no need to tell you what I'm like, because you're looking at me with those great dark eyes. But I'm never sure if other people, in the world, see me as I see myself. So I'll tell you what I *think* I'm like. You can tell me if you agree with the description.

I'm ten years old. Four feet six inches in height. With grey eyes and fair, straight hair. I'm wearing a blue shirt and blue jeans. I don't know why I'm not in my red swim suit as that was what I was wearing when I – well, never mind. But these clothes are more comfortable. I've got some freckles on my nose and I'm rather pale.

Oh, you wonder why I didn't say how heavy I am? Now that's a leading question. You're a sharp child. The fact is, I don't weigh anything at all. Not even as much as a feather. You see, I'm a ghost.

People usually look terrified at this point and run away. Sometimes they scream, and then I disappear because I can't bear loud noises. You don't look particularly scared and you haven't even said, 'Oh'! You say you guessed I might be a ghost because I didn't leave any footprints on the sand. That's very smart of you to notice. I think we shall get on well together.

I know your name is Dinah and I know why you are hiding in this sandy cove. I know, because I heard what was said on the beach. The other children wanted you to bathe with them but you didn't really want to. You said you had a headache. It wasn't true and the other children didn't

believe you. That's why they laughed in that horrid way. You didn't want to bathe because you're terrified of the sea. I have every sympathy with you. I'm no lover of the sea myself.

When I was born, there were two of us, Julia and Celia. We were identical twins. I was Julia. We did everything together and we looked exactly like each other, like two halves of an apple or two cherries on a stalk. We never quarrelled because we understood each other so well and we were never apart for more than a few minutes. At school, they thought we depended too much on each other and they put us in different classes so we could learn to be independent, but we cried so much they put us back in the same class, our desks touching.

Sometimes when we had tests, we made exactly the same

mistakes and the teacher said we copied each other. The class used to call us 'copy-cats'. But we didn't need to copy. Once, during exams, they put us in different rooms and we still got the same marks.

Yes, it's very nice being twins. You're always sure that at least one person in the world knows what you are really like, and you need never pretend to her. Children have to do a lot of pretending when they are young. We were spared that. Or I was.

Then, one day, the awful thing happened and we were separated. We were on this very beach, by the big green rocks. Celia had a cold and mother wouldn't let her bathe as the wind was in the east, blowing off the sea. So I went in by myself. The tide was low, as it is now, and I had to wade out a long way even to get wet up to my waist. I kept turning and waving to Celia and mother who were sitting on the beach and Celia kept waving back. Then, all of a sudden, the beach shelved and I was out of my depth. I couldn't swim and I waved frantically as I felt myself lose my footing and go under. Celia waved back, but she didn't

know I wasn't really waving – I was drowning. I remember swallowing water and choking but I don't remember much else. I learned afterwards that no one missed me at first because I was wearing a white cap that didn't show up.

Then people screamed and mother and Celia waded into the water with their clothes on, and a man came with a lifebelt. But when they got me out I was dead. They tried artificial respiration for an hour, but I never breathed again.

You want to know when I became a ghost? Why, from that very moment. I saw people giving my body the kiss of life and heard mother and Celia crying and saw a policeman keeping back the crowd that had gathered. He kept saying: 'Give her air! She needs air!' But by then I had all the air I needed. You might say I had turned into air.

Yes, I can do all the things that ghosts are supposed to do. I can walk through closed doors. Yes, I'll walk through that rock just to show you. Ah, that made you open your eyes, Dinah. But it's nothing. It's just my ghostly nature. We can't go against our natures. If you run into a rock you hurt yourself. But I let it pass through me.

You ask how Celia is getting on? Well, that's the sad part. She's much worse off than me. Of course she has father and mother and our two brothers, but it's me she needs. She's fifteen now and she hasn't a friend, not a real friend. I'm hoping she'll fall in love with some nice man later on and then she'll not feel so lonely.

Does she ever see me? Of course she does. Nearly all the time. But if she talks about me our parents get worried. They can't see me themselves so they think she is imagining things. They think she's crazy. They've taken her to see a great many doctors and once they shut her in a mental home for months. They said she suffered from delusions and that she was unbalanced and all kinds of things with long names. Schizo – something. Not a single doctor or nurse ever thought she might be haunted, not mad.

Why didn't I appear in front of the doctors so that they'd understand? Now that's beyond my power. I can only appear to people who believe in ghosts. And that means that I'm lonely, too. I was very fortunate to come across you this morning. I knew from the first that you would believe in me. And you did.

I must be going. If you don't mind my giving you some advice, I wouldn't tell anyone you've been talking to a ghost. They won't believe you. But they won't forget, either. They'll look at you as if you weren't all there. Or else they'll think you tell lies. So keep quiet if you want to be left in peace. Good-bye. I promised Celia I'd meet her by the bandstand.

Oh, you want to ask me one last question? Well, ask away. How long do I think I'll live? That's a difficult one to answer. I suppose you could say I wasn't alive now! There'll be nothing to keep me in this place when Celia dies. Perhaps we shall both go away together. Now I must be off. Good-bye again, Dinah. Good-bye!

Four Plus One

Rose and Ellen lived in an old house called The Old Rectory. Their father had lived there when he was a little boy. It had a steep, back staircase with wooden steps, and the children made a noise when they clattered up and down it, as well as a front one with a carpet and heavy, brass stair-rods. There were dark passages with twists and turns, and a large attic with a sloping ceiling where the children could make as much noise and mess as they liked. Rose and Ellen had been born there and to them it was just home. But when their cousins Jerry and Roger came to stay, they thought it was the most wonderful house they had ever been in, not at all like their own neat, bright bungalow on a new housing estate. It seemed like something out of a story book.

'Is there a ghost?' asked Jerry, who was nine. 'I do hope so.'

'I don't want to see it if there is one,' said Roger, who was three years younger.

'Of course there isn't a ghost!' laughed the girls. 'It's just an ordinary house, but nicer than most because it's our home,' added Rose.

'Good places for hide-and-seek,' said Ellen.

'And lots and lots of dark cupboards to shut people in,' said Rose.

'No! No! No!' shrieked Ellen, who was terrified of being shut up in the dark for even half a minute. Rose sometimes bundled her into a cupboard and shut the door, just to hear her scream – and she never failed to scream, loudly.

The four children played easily together. Sometimes the two older children split off, and sometimes the two younger, but they never divided into boys against girls. The boys introduced some new and exciting games, one of which was an outstanding sucess.

'Let's play at ghosts,' said Jeremy, when Roger and he had been staying at The Old Rectory for several days.

'How do we play it?' asked Rose.

'Oh, we have all the lights out and run about shrieking and waving our arms, and sometimes moaning.'

'It mustn't be all dark or I won't play,' said Ellen.

'Neither will I,' said Roger.

'Well, dark in places and light in places,' said Rose reasonably. 'Let's ask mother if we can play it after tea, when it's dark.'

When Mrs Nelson heard about the ghost game she said she would put a ten-watt bulb on the landing and a ten-watt bulb in the hall. 'Then you won't break your necks falling down stairs,' she explained. 'And I'll leave a proper light on in the kitchen, because the back stairs are so specially steep and dangerous.'

'You and uncle must shut yourself up in the study,' said Jeremy, 'then you'll have a little peace.'

'I doubt it,' said Mrs Nelson.

'And if you feel you'd like to come out and join in,' went on Jeremy, 'you can come out of the study and some horrible figure will spring out of the shadows, shrieking and moaning. That would be quite a thrill for you and uncle, wouldn't it?'

'A thrill we could well do without!' said Mrs Nelson. 'Now promise you won't fall down stairs –'

'We promise,' said the children.

'Or frighten the little ones –'

'But we want to be frightened,' said Ellen and Roger. 'We love being frightened. Please let them frighten us.'

'Oh, I give up!' said Mrs Nelson in despair. 'As long as

you frighten yourselves and leave John and me in peace, with the cat and the dog. We'd better keep the poor things with us.'

The children had a most satisfying game of ghosts after tea, and Ellen and Roger enjoyed it as much as the older ones. It became, at once, their favourite game. They decided to play it the next evening, too.

'May we dress up in old sheets and things, auntie?' asked Jeremy. 'It will be far more ghostly. We can jump out at people and scare them even more if we're draped in white. I shall make a noise like this.'

He made a loud shriek like a siren and let it slowly die away. The cat hid under the sofa and the dog barked angrily.

'I'll see what I can find,' said Mrs Nelson. 'I'll look out some sheets and a couple of old tablecloths.'

The children spent most of the day practising being ghosts. There were many problems to be dealt with. If they had the sheets right over their heads, they looked very ghost-like, but they could not see where they were going. Then the sheets seemed so very long and unmanageable and they kept walking on them and tripping up.

'It's a good thing we've practised in the light,' said Rose. 'I suppose real ghosts can see through sheets and things. Maybe they can't trip up or run into pieces of furniture.'

'Of course they can't,' said Roger, who suddenly appeared to know a great deal about the habits of ghosts. 'When they come to a chair – or a door – they simply walk through them.'

'Are they made of shadow?' asked Ellen. 'Or cloud? Or smoke?'

'No one knows,' said Rose mysteriously, 'but they certainly aren't flesh and blood like us. They can't bleed.'

'No one wants them to,' said Ellen quickly. 'A bleeding ghost – oh, that's horrible!'

'Some ghosts of dead kings carry their heads under their arms, if they were beheaded,' said Jeremy. 'I've never heard of any blood. Rose is quite right.'

'I hope you won't all have nightmares and call me in the night,' said Mrs Nelson. 'Do try to remember that ghosts aren't real. They are just made up to try and frighten silly people. They are pretence – like stories.'

'Are fairies real?' asked Ellen hopefully.

'Father Christmas isn't,' said Roger.

'He is in a way,' said Jeremy. 'I mean, our presents are real, so someone gives them to us.'

'But he doesn't come down the chimney,' said Roger. 'Think of all the houses like ours, with central heating. He couldn't, could he?'

'Are angels real?' asked Rose. 'I think they might be.'

'You'll have to make up your minds about these things when you get older,' said Mrs Nelson. 'You'll have to decide for yourselves. But remember – ghosts aren't real!'

When the children were alone together, Rose said firmly:

'Grown-ups don't know everything. Ghosts may be real. I'm sure some people have seen one, whatever our parents say.'

They had a long, interesting conversation about ghosts, as they practised draping themselves in their sheets. They found that a hood was best as it *looked* ghostly, but the wearer could see where he was going. They got quite expert at tucking in the folds round their feet, so they could walk.

'I can't wait for the ghost game,' said Roger. 'What a good thing we happened to be staying with you in this super old house. It wouldn't have been half the fun at home in the bungalow.'

'It's more fun for us, too,' said Rose. 'If it were just Ellen and me, then we'd always know who the other ghost was. Now it might be one of three people.'

Evening came at last. At six o'clock, Mr Nelson changed the bright bulbs on the landing and in the hall for dim ones. Though the children had been dressing-up all day, this felt different. This was the real thing. Even Jeremy, who was the oldest, felt shivers going down his spine when he saw a dim, white shape, muttering and bowing and waving long white arms, or felt a touch on the back of his neck and heard a moan in his ear.

As for Ellen and Roger, they trembled with joy and terror, and were ready to scream at anything at all, even their own pale shadow on the wall, or the whisk of white drapery.

It was difficult to believe that there were only four ghosts at large in the house. There seemed far more. They looked taller than they really were in their long robes, and it was impossible – at first – to be sure which ghost it was.

The back stairs were specially haunted, even with the dim light at the top and the bright light in the kitchen. They had taken their shoes off at the start, so their footsteps were noiseless. The whole affair was far better than they had hoped. Shrieks rang out when a ghost rose up from a dark corner, or jumped from behind a door with a dismal wail.

At last, Mr and Mrs Nelson said *they* had had enough excitement for one night, even if the children hadn't.

'Did you both enjoy your peaceful time in the study?' asked Jeremy, unwinding himself from a sheet which was now far from white.

'Peaceful time?' replied Mr Nelson. 'We never had a minute's peace. What with soothing the cat and pacifying the dog and trying not to jump out of our skins at every bump and scream, we had a pretty strenuous time. Now I'm going to make up for it and settle down with the paper. Good night, everybody, and not another sound till morning.'

'We couldn't settle to anything,' said Mrs Nelson, as she poured out their supper milk. 'I'm not usually nervous, but

the house seemed so creepy and strange, as if it were really haunted. No sound of footsteps or doors banging, just a few mysterious bumps. I looked out once and saw a tall, white figure glide across the hall, muttering to itself in a sinister way. I don't know who it was. It looked as tall as daddy.'

The children did not talk much while they had supper. Jeremy and Roger shared a room, and Jeremy had to do some reassuring before Roger could get off to sleep. To make doubly sure, he opened the door of the hanging cupboard to prove that it was empty, and he locked the bedroom door and put the key under his pillow.

The girls had a room each, so they could not talk to each other, but Ellen took her favourite doll to bed as well as her usual teddy bear, so she had something friendly on each side. She told her companions the story of the *Three Little Pigs*, and was asleep before the wolf fell into the pot.

The next day, the children slept later than usual, and Mr and Mrs Nelson had had their own breakfast when the children were ready for theirs.

'Here are your eggs, and a stack of toast, and there's honey and marmalade. I expect you're extra hungry after your energetic evening.' Mrs Nelson went off to do her shopping when she had seen the children started.

Rose said suddenly :

'I've been thinking about something ever since yesterday. I stayed awake for ages last night, thinking about the same thing. There ought to have been only four ghosts around the house. But I think – in fact I'm pretty sure – in fact I'm certain sure – that there was a fifth. An extra one. I saw it twice, once going into the bathroom and once coming out.'

'Did it make a sound ?' asked Jeremy.

'No, it was absolutely silent.'

'Then how did you know it wasn't one of us ?'

'It was different,' said Rose slowly. 'We all had hoods on, but this one hadn't. It had nothing on its head at all!'

'Then you could see its face?'

'Yes, but not very well. It was all white. Each time it fluttered away, once into the bathroom and once towards the back stairs. But it wasn't one of us.'

'I saw it too,' said Jeremy. 'I saw it when I went into the bathroom to hide behind the door. I must have disturbed it, as it came out at once. I don't know why, but I felt it was a child, a boy.'

'I thought it was a child too,' agreed Rose. 'Yes, a boy, I'm almost sure.'

'I saw it as well,' said Ellen. 'It was on the landing, looking kind of lost. It wasn't going anywhere special. I don't know where it went afterwards because I was so scared I got away first. I simply tore down the back stairs. I didn't say anything because I thought it must be one of you with your hood off. But I half-knew it wasn't. It was all white and glistening.'

'That's right,' said Jeremy. 'It was glistening, almost as if it shone in the dark.'

'I didn't see it,' said Roger sadly. 'I do wish I had.'

'You be thankful you didn't,' said Jeremy. 'I almost wish I hadn't seen it. But as three of us saw it, all separately, it proves that it was there. What do we do next?'

'Tell mummy and daddy,' said Rose promptly. 'They're very sensible and they never laugh at us, not even if they think we are silly.'

'What can they *do* about it?' asked Jeremy.

'It must be a ghost of somebody who was once alive. Probably someone who lived here. As daddy's parents lived here, and I think his grandparents, he might know who the ghost might be. That would be a great help. Ghosts often want someone or something to set their minds at rest. We might be able to find out what this one wants.'

'Are ghosts always unhappy?' asked Ellen.

'I don't know about always, but they often seem to be in books. Shall we talk to daddy now? He's in his study.'

'All right, if you're sure he'll take us seriously,' said Jeremy doubtfully.

They went into the study and Mr Nelson put down his pen at once.

'Daddy, we want to ask you something very important. Can you spare some time?'

'Of course, Rose.'

'We want to ask you about a ghost –'

'And about this house long ago –'

'And the people who lived here, even before you were born.'

'Ask what you like,' said Mr Nelson. 'Now, who'd like to begin?'

First Rose, and then Jeremy, and then Ellen, told all they could remember about the extra ghost. It took a long time. Then Mr Nelson spoke.

'All I can tell you is what my grandparents told me – they'd be your great-grandparents. Before they bought this house, some people with an only child lived here, an only boy. There was no bathroom in those days and what is now our bathroom, was the little boy's nursery. I once noticed some marks on the door and was told that perhaps the little boy made them, in a fit of temper.'

'Was there anything special about the little boy, uncle?' asked Jeremy. 'Anything sad?'

'Yes, there was. He fell off the swing and injured his back and the treatment, in those days, was months in bed at home, with the doctor calling. Nowadays he'd be in hospital. He may have had his bed moved into the playroom. I don't know. Anyhow, when he was walking about again, he fell down the back stairs and was so badly hurt that he died.

That's all I know and it isn't much. Now run away and get some fresh air.'

'What was his name, daddy?' asked Rose.

'Oh, I'm not sure. Something with an aitch – Harold or Hamish or something.'

'Please, please try to remember, daddy. You often say to us: "Think and it will come back".'

'So I do. Well, I will think and I'll tell you if I remember.'

'What do we next?' said Jeremy.

'We must try to see the ghost boy again, that's certain. If he was ill in bed all those weeks – perhaps months – his playroom must have been his whole world. No wonder he wants to see it again.'

'But supposing we never see him again?'

'Then that's too bad,' said Rose impatiently. 'When we see him again one of us must speak to him.'

'What shall we say?'

'I know,' said Ellen, bubbling with excitement. 'We know he wants his toys and we know he'll never find them in our bathroom. Why not show him where *our* playroom is, up in the attic?'

'And *our* toys,' broke in Rose.

'And we'll tell him he can play with them while we are asleep.'

'How pleased he'll be,' said Roger. 'That is, if he stays to listen and doesn't just fade away.'

'He may find some of your toys rather strange, if his were bought long ago. He won't understand space-ships and rockets and helicopters,' said Jeremy.

'The Noah's Ark will be all right,' said Ellen. 'That's in the bible.'

'And farm animals.'

'I've seen pictures of old-fashioned children with bats and balls and hoops and tops,' said Rose. 'We haven't a hoop.'

'We've lots of balls, though. And a top.'

During the rest of the day, the children talked incessantly of the ghost boy. What they would say to him. How they would make friends with him. What toys he would like. The only topic they didn't mention was what would happen if they never saw him again, or if they spoke to him and frightened him away for ever. But these possibilities were always at the back of their minds.

They decided to dress up as ghosts as before because he had first appeared when they were dressed that way. They chose Rose to speak to him as she lived in the house always, and she had seen him twice.

First, they went up into the attic where the girls kept most of their toys, and tidied it up. This took a long time as it was hardly ever tidied as the room was never used by any-one else. With the games put back in the boxes, things picked up from the floor, and the floor swept, the room was trans-formed.

Then after lunch, they went back again to arrange the room for the ghost visitor, if he could be persuaded to visit it. The rocking horse was dusted and his saddle put on properly. The Noah's Ark was put on the table under the window. The cupboards were left with the doors ajar so that they'd open at a touch. The drawers were left partly pulled out as well.

They kept adding last minute touches. Ellen left a colouring book open with crayons beside it. Rose found the picture book with old-fashioned pictures of girls in long dresses and sashes, and boys in sailor suits. The musical box was put beside a jack-in-the-box as they were both considered suit-able.

They looked round the room with great satisfaction, sure that the ghost boy would find something to his liking.

'We've made it look like a *real* playroom,' said Ellen proudly. 'It was rather a junky, rubbishy room before.'

'We can't tell what his own nursery was like,' said Rose. 'He may just want his own old toys and we haven't a clue what they were.'

'Oh, he'll be curious,' said Jeremy cheerfully. 'All children are curious and I expect ghost children are too. He'll want to open the drawers and cupboards just to find

out what's inside. And take the lid off boxes. And wind things up to make them go.'

At tea-time they asked Mrs Nelson if they could play ghosts again before they went to bed.

Mr and Mrs Nelson exchanged glances. They half guessed

what the children were planning to do, though they couldn't be sure.

'Very well,' said Mrs Nelson. 'Roger and Ellen, are you both certain you want to play?'

'Of course we do,' said Roger and Ellen, indignantly.

'Very well, you can play from six till seven. Daddy and I will be in the study as before. With the door open,' she added

'so if any one wants some light or warmth or company they can pop in and visit us.'

The children waited quietly till six o'clock, dressed in their white sheets. They had to decide where each one should be when the lights went out. If Rose waited upstairs alone, then the others would miss whatever happened. But four of them together might scare the ghost boy away. They decided in the end that Rose should lurk near the bathroom door, but not too near. The other three should sit on the top step of the back stairs. They could see the bathroom door by leaning back and craning their necks.

Rose was delighted when her father suddenly put his head out of the study and said 'Horace.'

'Horace what? Oh, I remember. Thank you, daddy. I mustn't forget, now. Horace. Horace. Horace.'

'I wonder if Horace is near us now, only invisible, listening to all we are saying,' said Jeremy.

'No,' said Ellen firmly. 'Ghosts only appear in the dark or in a dim light.'

'I'd rather he wasn't here,' agreed Roger. 'We don't want ghosts everywhere. It's not comfortable.'

At six o'clock the children took up their positions as arranged. Rose ran quickly up to the attic to turn the light on there or else it would have been pitch dark.

'I don't suppose Horace needs a light,' said Ellen. 'He can see in the dark.'

'Like cats,' added Roger.

'But I'm not a ghost or a cat. I'd bump into things,' said Rose.

'You might fall backwards down the stairs and break your neck, and then *you'd* be a ghost!' said Ellen.

Everyone laughed and felt better. Ghosts weren't so bad if you could make jokes about them.

Time passed. Rose took a few silent steps. The others sat still on their top step, proving that children can keep still

if they want to, still as stones. The hall clock struck a quarter past six. Roger sneezed. The cat came up to visit them, sniffed as if she could smell mice, lashed her tail violently, and then padded back to the study. Ellen got pins and needles and had to stand up to rub her leg. The clock struck half past six.

The next quarter of an hour was the longest. Sometimes they felt a sudden draught of air and wondered if someone, or something, had passed by. Stairs creaked. They wondered why. At first they had felt hot in their flowing robes, but now they felt cold and shivery. The idea of the warm, lighted study was attractive, at least to think of. The clock struck the three-quarters. Almost at once, things began to happen.

A slim, white shape appeared on the landing, at the head of the stairs, and fluttered uncertainly towards the bathroom. Rose moved into the doorway to block its path. She no longer felt cold or on edge. She was relieved and excited.

'Are you looking for your nursery, Horace?'

The white shape nodded.

'Well, you won't ever find it. It's gone. It's been turned into a bathroom. It's quite different now. Look for yourself!'

She stepped to one side and Horace floated through the door, turning his small, shining head.

'It's different, isn't it? Are you very sorry?'

Horace nodded again and brushed a small hand across his eyes. Rose hoped that ghosts couldn't cry. He managed to look bitterly disappointed without saying a word, and with his face covered by a white, transparent veil that showed the darkness of his eyes and the shape of a small, jutting nose.

'But we have a nursery of our own, my sister Ellen and me, up at the top of the house, and full of our toys. Shall I show it to you?'

Another ghostly nod.

'Come with me. It isn't far. Do come.'

Rose walked up the attic stairs and into the brightly lit playroom. She heard no sound of following footsteps, but she looked back once and saw Horace floating at her heels, on the next stair, closer than she had expected.

They went into the playroom together.

Horace drifted noiselessly about, once reaching out a pale arm towards the rocking horse, once bowing his head over a picture book.

'You can play with anything you like whenever you like,' said Rose. 'You can ride on Dobbin or build with our bricks or read our books. Or look at the pictures, if you can't read.' He seemed so small that she thought perhaps he couldn't read.

Horace shrank back into a shadowy corner and turned his head nervously. Rose was afraid he might disappear any moment as he looked so pale and his face less glistening. She longed to reassure him.

'It'll be perfectly all right. Once we're in bed no one ever comes up here, so you wouldn't be disturbed. And mummy and daddy don't mind. I mean, they wouldn't mind if they knew about you, though of course they don't.'

Horace came out of his corner and put his finger to his lips. Then he stretched out a ghostly arm and touched her lips. It was obvious that he wanted her to keep him a secret.

'Yes, I understand,' said Rose. 'You don't want grown-up people to know about you. I won't tell, ever. You mustn't mind Ellen knowing as its her playroom too, and Jeremy and Roger. They're children too. They're our cousins and very nice.'

A slight hesitation, and then the nod came.

The clock struck seven.

'I must go, because its our supper time. But do stay up here if you want. Please, please do.'

She ran downstairs and joined the excited group huddled

on the landing. They went back to the cosy, bright kitchen where Mrs Nelson had put out their supper. She looked from face to face as if trying to read their thoughts, and then she said:

'I'll leave you alone to eat what you want and then go up to bed. You look bursting with secrets.'

'So we are,' said Rose, 'but they're all nice ones. Nothing you wouldn't approve of.'

The second they were alone, the questions began.

'What did you do up in the attic?'

'Did he talk at all?'

'We could only hear your voice, but we saw him floating up the stairs behind you.'

'Did you leave him up there?'

At last there came a pause, and Rose said quickly:

'I'll tell you every single thing that happened if you don't interrupt and let me remember properly.'

There was complete silence. She could have heard a pin drop. She tried to recall everything that had happened, and the others helped by staying quiet till she had finished.

'So I left him there when the clock struck seven. He was a bit less frightened after I'd said I'd keep him a secret from the grown-ups. He was a brighter colour – well, a brighter white.'

Rose stopped and drank some milk.

'Are you sure he didn't say one word?' asked Jeremy. 'Didn't you hear his voice at all?'

'Not one word. Just nods and head shakes. It sounds queer now, but it seemed quite ordinary when we were talking.'

'But you said –' interrupted Ellen.

'I meant when I was talking to *him*. It was easy to see if he was pleased or upset. His whiteness altered. It got paler or brighter. And I didn't mind about him not actually speaking. It may sound silly now, but it was so beautifully easy and natural at the time.'

'What about when he touched your mouth?' asked Roger.

'It was such a tiny touch I hardly felt it, but I know he did. It was like thistledown – but cold thistledown. Very cold.'

'Like a snowflake?' suggested Roger.

'No, it wasn't wet. It was a kind of very slight tickle.' She put her hand to her mouth as if she could still feel it.

They went to bed with so much on their minds, that Jeremy and Roger thought they would talk about the ghost boy half the night. Ellen was equally sure she would never get to sleep, and she nearly asked if she could move into the little bed in her parents' room, where she or Rose occasionally slept if they were not well. But as it happened, all four children feel asleep in record time.

Only Mr and Mrs Nelson lay awake longer than usual.

'Don't worry so,' said Mr Nelson. 'After all, the children were peacefully asleep when we looked in at them. If they'd been distressed or frightened they would have called out, or come downstairs. You're just imagining things.'

'I suppose I am,' said Mrs Nelson. 'They were enthralled by what you told them about the little boy who died long ago and whose nursery is now our bathroom – and has been for many years. I think they were acting something about him.'

'A very good way of dealing with things they don't understand,' said her husband. 'Lots of their games have fears in them. They enjoy it. Think of cowboys and Indians and robbers, and now, perhaps, ghosts. It takes the terror away, and leaves the fun and excitement.'

'I suppose you're right,' said Mrs Nelson, settling for sleep.

The next morning, the boys came quietly into Rose's bedroom, fully dressed.

She woke in an instant.

'We couldn't wait to go and look at the attic,' said Jeremy, 'but he didn't want to go without you. Are you coming?'

'Yes,' said Rose, wide awake. 'But we must fetch Ellen. She'd never forgive me if she missed anything.'

Ellen woke as quickly as Rose, and both put on dressing-gowns. Rose was allowed to go into the attic first, as she had actually spoken to Horace. They all four walked round the room, observing and examining carefully.

'There's one thing we know,' said Ellen. 'Horace was – I mean is – a very tidy boy. Some boys would have turned everything upside down in no time. He's put everything back in its place.'

'If he ever got anything out!' said Roger. 'He may have just floated around and then gone away. We don't know. We never will know.'

'We know something already,' said Rose. 'I left this book on the table open at a picture of two children in sailor suits sailing a boat on a pond. But some pages have been turned over – quite a lot in fact. It's open now at a picture of a boy flying a kite, with a dog jumping up at the string.'

'Couldn't it have been the draught?' asked Jeremy.

'No, it couldn't. There's no window open. And the pages are thick because it is an old book. Mother says the pictures were drawn by someone called Kate Greenaway.'

'And we do know he can plait,' added Roger.

'Plait? How do you know? What did he plait?'

'Dobbin's tail, of course. He had a flowing tail yesterday. I noticed because I should like to have made it into a plait but I don't know how to do it.'

They all four looked at Dobbin. His tail was in a neat, thick, black plait.

'I told him he could ride on Dobbin, if he liked,' said Rose.

'And he *did* like,' said Ellen.

They thought he might have moved this or that, a box of counters or the bricks, but they couldn't be sure, as they were sure of the picture book and the rocking horse's tail.

The rest of the boys' visit went by in a flash. There were so

many things to do, and no time for them all. They often played in the attic if it were raining, and they always went there first thing in the morning, before breakfast. Once they found a little wooden horse and cart in the middle of the floor, and on one never-to-be-forgotten morning, they found a tall tower of bricks, taller than they themselves.

'He left it for us to see,' said Ellen. 'He likes us.'

The others hoped she was right. It was comforting to think that the little, lost ghost boy remembered them sometimes. They were sure that they would never forget *him*, as long as they lived.

The Weeping Witch

The village children had all heard stories of the Weeping
Witch, but these stories were always about people who had
lived long ago, and never about anyone who was alive now.
The stories usually began with: 'My grandmother once knew
someone who –' or even: 'My great-grandfather used to tell
how one evening –'

Sometimes the children forgot all about her for months
and months. Sometimes they talked about the stories and
wondered how they could see the Weeping Witch for themselves. Their fathers and mothers just laughed, and said:

'Surely you don't believe all that rubbish? There are no
witches left except in story books. Nor ghosts either!'

One day, Jane and Joanna were playing in the wood. It
was during the Christmas holidays and was getting dark,
though the church clock had just struck four o'clock.

'Let's go and see old Mrs Bobbin,' said Jane. 'There's her
cottage.'

'We'll take her a bundle of sticks for firewood,' said
Joanna. 'She's always glad of some.'

The little girls quickly gathered an armful of sticks each,
especially ash and oak which burned well.

'I know why you want to visit Mrs Bobbin,' said Joanna.
'It isn't to give her the sticks. It's because you hope she'll tell
us about the Weeping Witch.'

'Well, what if it is? Don't you want to know?'

'Yes, but father and mother say it's all nonsense. Though

we may as well take her the sticks now we've gathered them.'

They knocked on Mrs Bobbin's door and she asked them to come in. They laid the sticks on the hearth to get quite dry.

'Mrs Bobbin,' said Jane, 'do tell us the story about the Weeping Witch?'

'Please please do,' added Joanna. 'We like hearing about her.'

'It was a long time ago, a very, very long time ago,' began Mrs Bobbin, 'when I was a little girl in pinafores, smaller than you. People use to meet an old woman in the wood, at dusk, and she would be crying and wringing her hands, begging whoever it was to help her because she was in such trouble.'

'Did they help her?' asked Jane.

'The sensible ones hurried home as fast as they could, but sometimes someone would be sorry for her, and go off with her.'

'Then what happened?'

'That no one ever found out,' said Mrs Bobbin. 'They were never seen again.'

'But they couldn't just disappear,' said Jane. 'They must have come back sometime. People can't vanish away like a puff of smoke!'

Mrs Bobbin poked the fire and drew the curtains.

'No they couldn't, could they? It was all a pack of nonsense. Thank you again for the sticks, and you'd better be getting home or your mother will be after you.'

'Good-bye, Mrs Bobbin. Good-bye!' said the children, and hurried off. The lights were already twinkling in the cottage windows.

A few days later, Jane and Joanna were playing in the wood again. It was a friendly wood, with paths in it, and all the children played there. Mrs Bobbin's cottage was the only house, but the village street was only five minutes

away, where bicycles and cars passed, and mothers with prams.

The other children had aleady gone home, and Jane and Joanna stayed to finish a moss garden they were making between the roots of an oak tree.

'I've got two toadstools to plant in the moss,' said Jane.

'Oh good. They'll do for tables.'

'Or umbrellas.'

Just then they noticed someone watching them. She was a very old lady, as old as Mrs Bobbin, dressed in black clothes. The odd thing was that tears were pouring down her cheeks, and she did not bother to wipe them away.

'Oh, I'm in such dreadful trouble,' said the old lady. 'If no one helps me, I don't know whatever I shall do!'

'How can we help you?' said Jane.

'If you and your sister will come with me, I'll soon show you.'

'Haven't you any neighbours?' asked Joanna. 'Can't they help you? A grown-up would be sure to know what to do. They'd be better than a child.'

'No neighbours!' sighed the old lady, 'No neighbours, and no friends. I'm just a lonely old woman with no one to do a hand's turn for me.'

'*Where* do you want us to go?' said Jane, in a matter-of-fact voice. 'We live here and we know everybody in the village. But I've never seen you before.'

'It's only a little way – only a few steps and we're there,' said the old lady. 'Just as far as the fence.'

The fence marked the edge of the wood and the girls could see it in the dusk. It needed painting, but it had once been white.

'I'll come as far as the fence but not a step further,' said Joanna. 'It's tea-time, and mother will get worried.'

'Don't go! Don't go!' whispered Jane. 'She's the Weeping Witch, I know she is. Please, please don't go.'

'Rubbish!' whispered back Joanna. 'She only a poor old lady and she's upset about something. Stay where you are, if you're scared.'

'I am scared, I'm very scared. But if you go, I'm coming. I won't let you go alone.'

The old lady was now hobbling towards the fence, the children following.

'Climb on to the rail, my dears, and look over the field. You'll see where I live then.' They climbed on the rail and looked.

'There's only the scarecrow,' said Jane. 'He's nothing to be afraid of. He's stuffed with straw.'

Then, in a second, the old lady leapt lightly on to the rail in front of them, and some small, dark animal jumped up behind.

'Hold tight! Hold tight! We're off!' said the old lady, and the piece of what they thought had been railing sailed up into the air, smoothly and swiftly.

'You're the Weeping Witch,' shouted Jane, 'and this is your broomstick. Take us down at once. Take us home.'

She lifted one hand to clutch the old woman's arm, but found that she needed both hands to hold on with. The ground already looked a long way below.

Afterwards, the girls could never remember much about their ride.

'The bristly part of the broomstick was behind me,' said Joanna, 'and the black cat clung on to the bristles. I looked round once and saw his eyes like green lights.'

The children were too frightened to enjoy rushing through the air in this way, high above the trees and the telegraph posts, and they were glad when the broomstick came gently down in the garden of a cottage.

'Come in,' said the Witch. Her tears were all dried, and she looked pleased with herself. 'Come in to my cosy little home. I'm sure you'll be comfortable.'

The children soon found that the Weeping Witch's idea

of a snug house was very different from theirs. The floor was of cold stone. The table was bare. The chairs had straight, hard backs. There were cobwebs everywhere. The fire was the most cheerful thing, though it was nearly out, and only showed a glimmer of red.

The Witch lit several candles and changed into her slippers which were lined with fur. As she did this, she gave a stream of orders to the broomstick, who skipped about so fast that the girls could hardly follow him with their eyes.

'Broomstick, poke the fire.'

'Broomstick, sweep the floor. You see we have visitors.'

'Broomstick, make the soup.'

'Broomstick, brush up the hearth.'

'Broomstick, shake the door mat.'

By the time the Witch had warmed her feet by the fire, and the cat had licked each of her paws in turn, all these jobs were done. The soup was the colour of mud, with bits of green stuff floating in it. The girls ate every drop in their bowls because they dared not leave it.

After supper they were given a box of oddments to play with, bones and stones and shells and oak apples. They pretended to play with these, but really they were listening to the Witch talking to the cat.

'Cat,' she said. 'I will now tell you my plans. Joanna is the kinder of the two girls as it was she who offered to help me first. Jane just followed her. I shall let Joanna make needlework pictures with wool, which I shall hang on the wall. In the end the wall will be covered with pictures, so I can walk round enjoying them when I've nothing else to do.

'Jane, who isn't so kind, can work in the garden. I am sure we could grow many more nettles, thistles, and dandelions, and other things that I like. To start with, she can dig it over.'

'I hate needlework!' whispered Joanna.

'And I detest gardening!' whispered Jane.

'What will happen if they don't want to make needle-work pictures, or to grow nettles,' asked the cat.

'You know I never waste anything,' said the Witch. 'I shall turn them into anything I happen to need at the moment. A record player would be nice, or a new cloak.'

Long after the Witch and the cat were asleep, the children lay awake. The broomstick swept silently across the floor to the bed that they shared.

'Don't be unhappy,' he whispered. 'I'll help you when I have time. We'll have some fun together when the Witch and the cat are out.'

'I've got an even better idea,' said Jane. 'You work like a slave here, and I don't suppose you get a paid for it?'

'Not a penny! Not a penny!' sighed the broomstick.

'Then come home with us. You can just stand in the warmest corner of the kitchen, and you needn't do any work at all. If you get tired of being indoors, you can sweep up a few leaves in the garden. And once a year you'll be shampooed with lovely soap-suds and put out to dry in the sun.'

The broomstick began to shake with excitement and all his bristles danced with joy.

'No work!' he quavered. 'A real shampoo! Just stand in the corner and watch other people doing things! What bliss!'

'You deserve a good rest,' said Joanna.

'Perhaps I do. I work all day and half the night – And the cat sharpens her claws on me – And the witch loves going out in thunder storms and in snow, and I'm always catching cold.'

'Let's go now, this very minute,' said Jane. 'Tell us how best to escape from this horrid place. Snug and comfortable, indeed!'

'I've picked up a few words of magic during the years I've lived here,' said the broomstick. 'Enough to get us away, I'm sure.'

Open up, door,
Without creak or groan,
And don't tell the Witch
That the birds have flown

The door did what it was told, without creak or groan, and soon the girls were speeding through the air towards home, holding on to the faithful broomstick. They loved the ride this time, as they knew they were safe.

The broomstick was happier than he dreamed he could ever be, in the corner of the kitchen. He had such a kind heart that he was always helping, even though he was not expected to work. If the girls were late in the morning, he set the table in a twinkling, and scurried around looking for their books or for lost gloves.

He loved being shampooed in soap-suds and he never caught another cold. Best of all, he knew hundreds of magical stories which he had learned from reading the Witch's Spell Book, and was always ready to tell them to Jane and Joanna.

Ghosts at Shield-on-the-Wall

The three children stopped while Dorothy spread out the map on the ground. Jules, next to her in age, flung off his rucksack and flopped down, resting his head on it. Magnus, three years younger, knelt beside her, following the blade of grass which she was using as a pointer.

'We're just here, at Shield-on-the-Wall.'

'I'm not going any further,' said Jules rebelliously. 'I've gone far enough. These blasted tent poles have been digging into my back for ages.'

'As it happens, you won't have to,' said Dorothy calmly. 'We're going to camp here. This lake will do for washing and it's probably O.K. for tea when it's boiled. The line of the Wall will be a shelter. It's ideal. And so beautiful.'

They all looked over the landscape bathed in the evening light. The shadows were already lengthening as the sun declined over to the west by Sewing Shield, beyond the few trees. They were in Northumberland, not far from a main road, but there was no sound of traffic. In the distance, the Roman Wall stretched its long, broken line across their view, rising and falling over the landscape.

'Aren't you glad you came?' asked Dorothy, unstrapping her rucksack. She was a tall, thin girl with her long hair, for the moment, tied back with a piece of tape.

'Yes, I am,' said Magnus, who was small for aged twelve. 'I wouldn't have missed this for worlds. I didn't know there

were such lovely, wild, lonely places in England. All this –'

He turned his head slowly to take in the wide sweep of the view.

'I'm glad, too,' said Jules. 'Very very glad.'

'We ought all to be thankful that my history course included Roman Britain, and that Miss Jago is such a super teacher,' said Dorothy.

'And that you're so mad keen on her,' said Jules.

'And that you're a Queen Guide,' said Magnus.

'And that daddy agreed to let us have a camping holiday on our own,' added Dorothy. 'It was odd that mummy, who is so nervous about colds and germs and things, never turned

a hair at the prospect of our sleeping out, or hitching a lift, or being gored by a bull.'

'Or pestered by nasty men!' put in Jules.

'Yes, it was daddy who kept hinting at unpleasant experiences and got quite embarrassed when we asked him exactly what unpleasant experiences he had in mind.'

'I think mum's always on our side,' said Magnus. 'She was so strictly brought up in her convent that she likes us to do all the things she wasn't allowed to. She was jolly decent to let Jules and me go up that mountain in Wales on our own and she never minded when I fell in a bog and came home coated with mud.'

'No, she didn't,' said Jules. 'She just said: "Drop your clothes in the bath and go for a swim." '

'But daddy was furious because you made her all that extra work when she was supposed to be having a holiday. When I'm married, I shall expect my husband to grumble if the children make lots of extra work. But of course, by that time, husbands may do things like washing the children's clothes which they don't do now. Or only in emergencies.'

'Women's Lib for ever!' said Jules, more out of habit than with intent to annoy.

They chose a site and soon put up the two light tents, one for the two boys and the other for Dorothy, who kept the stores and cooking things along one side of hers. Soon the two primuses were roaring away behind their wind-breaks, though it was a calm evening. Tea was made with well-boiled water from the lake, and sausages and bacon were soon sizzling in the frying pan.

'I wish we'd been able to buy a sliced loaf,' said Jules, hacking thick wedges off some crusty bread.

'I prefer it like this,' said Magnus. 'Thick bread needs thick butter and that's how I like it.'

They finished their supper with bananas and apples.

'I needn't clean my teeth as I've eaten my apple last,' said Magnus contentedly. 'Is this hollow the vallum or the ditch, Dorothy?'

'The vallum, of course, on the south of the Wall. And over there was the next milecastle.'

'I forget what you said milecastles were for,' said Jules, wiping out the pan with a wad of grass.

'For housing the troops that patrolled the Wall. The Romans built them every mile but their miles were a little shorter than ours.'

'The Romans had a jolly easy time living on the Wall,' said Jules. 'I suppose they had much better food and armour

and weapons than the poor old Britons, so they always came off best in a scrap.'

'They had shields and spears and short swords,' said Dorothy, 'and of course helmets. But it wasn't much fun for them, being a Wall soldier. Lots of them came from Spain and Italy and they must have been appalled by the long, cold winters. They may never have seen snow before. And I suppose they had wives and children thousands of miles away. They must have dreaded being posted here. Like being sent to Siberia. Auden wrote a poem about one of them which begins:

> *Over the heather the wet wind blows,*
> *I've lice in my tunic and a cold in my nose.*
> *The rain comes pattering out of the sky,*
> *I'm a Wall soldier, I don't know why.*

'Auden is a – '

'No, hold it! Don't tell us!' begged Jules. 'We're not complete morons. Auden was a poet.'

The children went for a walk round the lake which would have been very boggy underfoot if the weather hadn't been dry recently. Clouds of midges danced over the water.

'Gosh, I'm being eaten alive!' said Dorothy. 'They're biting through my jersey.'

'They must like the smell of that anti-fly stuff mother gave us,' said Jules, scratching in despair. 'I'm drenched in the stuff but they're all in my hair.'

'We'll get into bed quickly and get well down in our sleeping bags,' said Dorothy. 'That's the best cure. Come along, you two.'

They were soon asleep as they were used to sleeping out in the garden at home. The moon rose on a peaceful scene, reflected in the shallow lake where occasionally a ripple appeared on the smooth water, and died away silently.

Dorothy was having a horrible dream in which people

were shouting and running, when she woke to find it was true. Rough voices were calling out in a strange language, and other voices were uttering cries of fear and pain. The tent shook as Magnus hurled himself down beside her, trembling, and Jules followed close behind.

'What is it?' said Dorothy, putting an arm round Magnus's shaking body. 'What's wrong?'

'There are lots of men outside, on the Wall and down near the camp. And I think there are animals,' whispered Jules.

They could hear the lowing and snorting of cattle and the trampling of hoofs. A dog barked frantically. The tent shook as something – or someone – collided with the side. A man cursed loudly.

Magnus kept his face hidden, trembling and occasionally moaning with terror. Dorothy patted his shoulder and stroked his hair. She felt wide awake and though she was frightend and bewildered, she was alert.

'Hold the flap back,' she said to Jules, who did so and they both looked out of the tent doorway.

Dark in the bright moonlight, they saw the shapes of men in armour, leaping down from the Wall and grappling with other men who appeared to have no armour except swords or perhaps sticks. The armoured ones kept shouting in a strange language, short, sharp, words like orders. She heard the word 'latrones' repeated several times. Hand-to-hand fighting was going on and she and Jules knew that people were being hurt, perhaps killed. They saw bodies on the ground. A little way away, cattle were bunching together and some of the soldiers set off in pursuit.

Then came shouts of relief and a few cheers rose as a detachment of horsemen approached the cattle, riding in an orderly way along the vallum. Some of the men without helmets ran off, followed by the soldiers, but a sharp word of command brought the soldiers back. The cavalry were left to look after any stragglers.

Magnus's eyes stayed tight shut, but Dorothy and Jules watched every move.

'Look!' said Jules. A dark shape was crawling on its stomach towards the tent. They never thought that their lives might be in danger. This was someone seeking refuge – perhaps wounded. Jules held the flap of the tent well back and the figure crawled slowly and painfully inside. Jules closed the flaps and skewered them firmly down.

'The torch –' said Dorothy.

Jules switched on the large car torch they kept near them at night for emergencies, and both looked at the stranger. Magnus sat up straight and opened his eyes for the first time.

'He's only a boy,' said Jules.

'He's bleeding to death,' said Magnus, shuddering.

They saw the boy had left a wet, dark, sticky trail behind him. He lay still when the tent flaps had been closed, panting for breath. The children saw that the blood was welling fast from a wound just above the knee.

'Get the wide bandage from the First Aid Box, Magnus,' said Dorothy. 'It's just beside you.'

While Magnus found the box and opened the lid and took out the wide, crêpe bandage supplied by their mother in case of a sprained ankle or wrist, Dorothy looked at the wound.

'There's something sticking in it,' she whispered. 'Perhaps the tip of a weapon. Hold his hand tightly while I pull it out.'

Jules took hold of the thin brown hand, which felt hot and rough to his touch, and gripped it. The fingers returned the grip, and the man tried to stifle a groan as Dorothy extracted the metal tip of a spear, with a few inches of broken wooden shaft attached.

'That's very good,' Dorothy whispered. 'You're very brave. Just breathe deeply and relax. It'll all be over soon. Just let yourself relax. Don't try to sit up.' She pressed gently on his shoulders to show him what she meant.

'Lint, please, Magnus. That roll of pink fluffy stuff. And the scissors.'

She folded the lint several times to make a thick pad and pressed it on the wound. Then she bandaged firmly over it, round and round the leg, pulling tightly each time she passed the bandage round.

'Drink,' she said to Jules, who found there was still some cold tea left in the tea-pot which they had forgotten to empty.

'Give it to me. I'll feed him through the spout.' Dorothy raised the man's head and put the spout to his mouth. He drank steadily.

'Sugar lumps, please. In the packet.'

Jules found the packet and put one in his mouth. He began to suck it noisily.

'Give him more when he's finished that one. It's good for shock. And cover him with my sleeping bag.'

The wounded man repeated some words in a strange

language and smiled. It was clear that he was thanking them. The children smiled back, even Magnus who had stopped shivering and was longing to be helpful.

The man was now as comfortable as the children knew how to make him. He had two of Dorothy's jerseys rolled up for a pillow, and her jeans rolled under the knee of the injured leg to support it. The sleeping bag was keeping him warm and Jules gave him sips of cold tea and a sugar lump alternately.

Once or twice he tried to sit up and said something that sounded urgent, but Dorothy pushed his shoulders firmly back and put her fingers to her lips.

The shouts and noises outside had died down, but later the troop of horsemen galloped back. The wounded man muttered something and Dorothy thought she caught the word 'Carrawburgh'.

'I believe he means that there was some cavalry stationed at Carrawburgh and they've come back to report.'

'I'll look out,' said Jules.

'No, please don't. Someone may see us. Though I don't understand how. *We* can see *them* and yet they can't see the tents.'

'Do you mean they aren't really there?' said Magnus. 'But we're here, aren't we? I don't like it much.'

'Nor do I. But we're here, all right, and together. And so is the wounded Briton.'

'And what about the ones in armour with shields and helmets?' asked Jules.

'Well, we know one of them wounded this poor man, didn't he? But I daresay the Britons were on a raid. I know they used to steal cattle if they got a chance.'

'They didn't pull it off this time.'

Dorothy soaked her handkerchief in some water from the canvas bucket and wiped the Briton's face and then laid the wet handkerchief on his forehead. They sat in silence. Once

the horses had galloped off there was no sound except the lowing of the cattle who were slow to settle down.

Magnus began to nod and sat close to Jules to try to keep warm. They had switched the torch off to save the battery. Dorothy flashed it on occasionally to look at her watch and to see how the patient was. He looked a better colour and his eyes were always wide open and alert, searching her face, bright blue under a mop of shaggy fair hair. He was very young. Probably no older than herself. When her watch said four o'clock she allowed him to sit up and move a little.

'Give him something to eat,' she said to Jules. 'Anything you can find.'

Jules offered him four digestive biscuits and two sausages, which he ate quickly, and then an apple. He seemed pleased to see the apple and crunched it up, core and all.

They unpegged the flaps of the tent and he looked cautiously out. There was no one in sight. He lifted his hand in farewell and the children shook hands and wished him good luck. When he realised that this was their form of leave-taking he shook hands again and again, smiling and showing his strong white teeth.

Dorothy looked at the bandage. The blood was beginning to seep through but she dared not interfere with it or she might make things worse.

With further handshakes – a prolonged one for Dorothy – he crept away into the morning twilight, agile as a cat.

The boys went back to their tent, Magnus only half-awake, but just able to fumble his arms into the sleeves of the jersey that Dorothy held out. They were asleep in a few minutes.

Dorothy wriggled into her sleeping bag, adding a jersey and socks on top of her pyjamas. But the bag was comfortably warm from its contact with the wounded Briton. Words poured through her mind, milecastle, Carrawburgh, vallum, ditch, with blurred images following each other. Sleep seemed impossible with so much to think of, but the

next thing she knew was some walkers were passing the camp and calling out 'Good morning'.

She sat up and looked at the world outside. She saw brilliant sunshine and the group that was passing, whistling and singing, was composed of boys and girls of her own age, in jeans with shirt sleeves rolled up.

She called back 'good morning' cheerfully and quickly scrambled into her clothes. It was nearly ten o'clock. She had slept like a log.

She woke the boys and soon they were eating their breakfast of cornflakes, chunks of bread and jam, and bananas. Jules boiled a billycan of water and made tea. As they drank it, the sun hot on their heads, they talked about the events of the previous night, which now seemed far away and incredible.

'Did it really happen, really and truly?' asked Magnus.

'Look into my tent,' said Dorothy briefly. The boys looked and saw the dark stain on the ground sheet. Dorothy dragged the sheet out on to the grass and sponged it with cold water. Soon it was only wet. Something fell off as she draped it on a rock to dry.

'The broken spear!' said Jules, pouncing on it. 'But it looks so different. So – so old. The wood is crumbling and the metal is almost rusted away.'

'It broke off about sixteen or seventeen centuries ago,' said Dorothy. 'No wonder it looks old. The miracle is that it survived at all. I shall keep it.' She wrapped it very carefully in a paper bag and put in the front pocket of her rucksack.

They went on resting in the sunshine, warm and together, before striking camp. Dorothy pored over the map.

'Where are we going today, Dorothy?'

'Vindolanda – it's about four miles. We'll have lunch on the way as we've had such a late breakfast.'

Whatever they talked about as they went on their way, whether it were rations or short cuts or curlews, it ended in

their discussing the night's adventures. All topics led to it.

'All roads lead to Rome,' thought Dorothy, 'or at least to Roman Britain.'

They showed the spearhead to the custodian at the Vindolanda museum, and he asked to keep it and have it properly identified. He noted down their names and address and the exact place where it had been found. A group of children no older than Dorothy were excavating near by, examining the ruins of the old Roman supply town that had flourished when the Wall was new and unbroken.

They studied the objects in the museum, the coins and fragments of sandals and bits of pottery. They also bought another book about the Wall, and Magnus bought a biro with VINDOLANDA written on it. This pleased him and he at once chose a picture postcard and sat down to write it to his mother. The other two did the same.

When they came back to Vindolanda with their parents, three years later, their spearhead was in a glass case too, with a card stating that it had been found at Shield-on-the-Wall. By then, Dorothy was at a university reading ancient history, preparing for the day when she would be an archaeologist and dig up the past.

But even if she had a life-time of learning ahead of her, she never expected to have another glimpse of the past such as she and Jules and Magnus had had on that moonlit night at Shield-on-the-Wall. The face of the wounded boy with his blue gaze and tangled fair hair remained clearer and nearer than any work she was doing; more eloquent than words on a page, more immediate than the fragments of pottery under her fingers.

Hadrian's Wall, built about AD 122–126, runs from Wallsend-on-Tyne to Bowness-on-Solway, a distance of about 73 miles. It consists mainly of (a) the Wall itself (b) a deep ditch close

to the Wall on the north side (c) a wide, shallow trench called the Vallum a little way south of the Wall (d) a Military Way running between the Wall and the Vallum.

Every few miles along the Wall was a substantial fort or camp; and at every Roman mile (1620 yds) was a Milecastle and between each Milecastle were two manned turrets.

Brownie

In the winter, the village of Haven was quiet as its name. The curving sweep of the beach was deserted except for sea-gulls and an occasional stray dog. The little hotels and boarding houses along the front, mostly painted white with blue-grey roofs, looked shut up. The whole place looked what it was – half alive, or asleep.

But Haven came to life in the summer. The beach was never crowded, but every patch of sand was decorated with castles and the prints of bare feet. Windows were wide open. Bathing towels flapped in the breeze. Bathing suits were spread out to dry in convenient places. At night, sounds of music and laughter drifted into the darkness, and gaily coloured cars filled the little car park.

Among the families who loved Haven and stayed there year after year for their holidays, was a collection of children known to outsiders, and to themselves, as The Group. They were boys and girls of various ages, often meeting on the sand dunes at one end of the front, and always doing things together. Sometimes it was obvious what they were doing, if it were rounders or cricket or kite-flying. Sometimes it seemed as if they were doing nothing at all, just standing around and staring.

But though The Group looked haphazard, as if it might dissolve at any moment, it was held together by strong ties. The strongest, perhaps, was habit. There was the habit of coming to Haven year after year during the summer holidays, something looked forward to for months in advance. Then

there was Gilly herself, the leader of The Group, whose mind threw up an unfailing series of ideas that, the moment they were explained, seemed so right, so suitable, that the other children adopted them at once.

Gilly was tall and red haired and had three small, freckled brothers, tough and energetic and silent. Then there were the three Ts, a family named Tabby and Toby and Thomas. They stayed with their aunt and their cousins Paula and Nicola. There were always odd children who simply appeared at the edge of the group, uncertain whether to hang around, or to go away. Gilly always took pity on them and said, in her friendly way, 'Would you like to play with us?'

Quickly the newcomers learned the names of the other children and revealed their own. The rules of The Group were not explained but they were quickly learned, too. The first rule was never to make a fuss if you were out. The second meant bowling easy balls to the little ones, and not finding them too quickly if they were playing hide-and-seek. There were others that could only be learned by waiting and watching.

Parents hardly entered into The Group's doings, but they were always in the background, to be placated and, when possible, obeyed.

Gilly and her brother had a tall, absent-minded mother who appeared to take very little notice of her family, but was adored by them. Their father made brief, dramatic appearances at weekends, dressed in a dark suit and sun glasses, and occasionally presenting The Group with not one – but *three* – rounders bats, and what seemed like miles of strong white string for their kites. Then he would disappear, not waiting to be thanked. A satisfactory father, on the whole.

The Group seldom met before ten o'clock in the morning, as breakfast was never before nine at the hotel and the boarding houses. Envy was felt for the three Ts, whose aunt

gave them breakfast at any time they liked, if she were awake herself. They met on the sand dunes where there were a few tumbledown bathing huts. There was a rickety wooden railing, of no apparent use, and as The Group arrived, they perched on this railing like a row of strange birds, Gilly and her brothers in navy blue, the others in all

colours. Everyone wore a jersey as there was always a fresh breeze off the sea. As a haven, it was by no means windless.

That morning, Gilly and her brothers arrived last.

'Has anyone looked in the letter-box?' asked Gilly.

No one had, but Paula jumped off the rail and put her hand down a rabbit hole that ran under one of the huts.

'Nothing there,' she said. The hole was used for such urgent messages as 'Had to go out today' or 'Relations arriving for lunch.'

The Group fixed their eyes on Gilly, expectantly.

'It's time the little ones chose. The tide is too low for a bathe this morning.'

'Hide-and-seek,' piped several voices.

'Let's find out who's "he",' and Gilly began the counting

rhyme, 'Piggy on the railway.' Then stopped, and said to a boy who was standing a little way off, 'Want to play?'

'Oh, yes please.'

The Group turned and had a good look at him. He had the deepest, darkest, most spectacular sun-tan they had ever seen. His hair was very fair, but his face and arms and legs were like polished wood.

One of Gilly's brothers, Marky, was 'he' and covered his eyes while the others hid. It was not such a bad spot for hiding places as might be imagined. There were the ruined bathing huts and some sprawling bushes and natural hollows in the sand. After an exciting game, during which they discovered the brown boy could run like the wind, there was just one person still to find. This was Tabby, the eldest of the three Ts.

'I've looked everywhere,' said Marky in despair, 'and not a sign of her.'

'She's in the end bathing hut,' said the brown boy.

'How do you know?'

'Anyhow, I've looked there,' said Marky promptly. 'I went all along the row.'

'Did you go inside?'

'Yes, inside each one.'

'Why not look again?'

The brown boy's voice was so friendly, that Marky didn't answer rudely as he might otherwise have done. He just said:

'I'll look again.'

He ran to the end bathing hut – looked inside – and was back in a second.

'No go.'

'Won't you try again? I would, if I were you.'

Marky, with rather a sulky expression on his face, tried again and went right inside. There were shouts as Tabby burst out and ran for home.

'It was the door,' panted Marky. 'It opened inward and I had to lift it, it was broken. Tabby stood behind the door, flattened against the wall. A marvellous place.'

By the end of the morning, the new member of The Group had become first Brown Boy, and then Brownie, and Brownie he stayed, even after they'd learned his real name, which was Brian.

After only one day with Brownie, The Group took to him. He was good at everything, throwing and catching and running. When they bathed in the afternoon, with the usual party of parents in attendance to see that the children took no risks and didn't stay in too long, Brownie was found to swim strongly and fast, and he didn't in the least mind holding up the chins of the small beginners.

'Your parents don't mind your bathing without them?'

Gilly asked. 'Mostly they want to come and watch. And fuss,' she added. 'My mother does.'

'No, they don't mind,' said Brownie. Gilly thought he sounded sad and she looked at him carefully. But his face was composed and cheerful.

Brownie fitted in with The Group so well that almost at once the other members forgot he was new and inexperienced. They began to consult him and he soon became Gilly's right-hand man. But he never pushed himself forward or spoke loudly. In fact, he seldom spoke at all unless someone asked him a question.

Occasionally the elder members went for a long walk over the far side of Haven. Their objective was the Haven golf course, which ran alongside the low cliffs that backed on to the beach. It was said by golfers to be a sporting course. The children were not interested in the course except for the fact that it resulted in a fair number of lost balls. The rough grass and bushes on the edge of the cliff, with little sandy paths and hollows, were a hazard. Balls often disappeared for ever down a sandy hole or under a prickly gorse bush, and players had to give up the search after poking and prodding for as long a time as they could spare.

The Group enjoyed a golf ball hunt and were satisfied if they found a couple of balls, however old.

One sunny, windy morning, having left the little ones to play on the beach, the older members set off for the golf links. The little ones, as usual, were unwilling to be left behind, but Gilly suggested a sand castle competition, and Brownie volunteered to give a prize for the best castle.

'What is the prize?' clamoured the castle builders.

'I don't know yet,' said Brownie, 'till I've seen the finished castles. But it will be a real prize.'

'What will the prize be?' asked Gilly, as they plodded along the beach.

'Oh, I'll find something,' said Brownie airily.

At last they reached the far side of Haven and climbed the low craggy cliffs on to the wild strip of land that bordered the links on the sea side. It was sheltered among the bushes and very hot in the sun. They poked around, sometimes stopping to watch a distant golfer drive off. Later they came upon two golfers beating the undergrowth.

'Hi, there!' called one. 'Have you children a few minutes to spare? I've just lost a brand new ball somewhere near here. It must be pretty near as I followed it with my eye.'

'Have you searched that patch of restharrow?' asked Brownie.

'Rest-what?'

'Restharrow. That pink flower over there.'

'Yes, I've looked there.'

Brownie walked to the flowery patch, stooped swiftly, picked up something and handed it to the golfer, who looked extremely surprised.

'Thank you. I must need glasses not to have spotted it. Thanks a lot.'

The golfers returned to their game.

'Did you see the ball straight away?' said Paula curiously. 'You were so quick.'

'Yes. Well, no.'

'Don't tease. I only asked a simple question. The answer can't be "yes" and "no".'

'But it is,' said Brownie. 'I felt sure the ball was there but I didn't actually see it till I looked.'

'Can you see things that other people can't?' asked Paula.

Brownie seemed uncomfortable, but he tried not to show it.

'Not exactly, only I'm rather good at finding lost things. That's all.'

'And lost people,' said Tabby with a laugh. 'You found me in the bathing hut though Marky had missed me twice.

He only looked the third time because you told him to. Did you see me go in there to hide? I suppose you must have.'

'Oh, no. I didn't *see* you go anywhere. I just knew.'

Brownie changed the subject and soon after found a rather old ball down a hole.

'Here's one prize for the castle competition,' he said. 'Now I only want three more.'

'A prize for everyone?' said Gilly.

'Of course. People always like to win prizes, especially when they're young.'

'You're not so old yourself!' remarked Gilly.

'Perhaps I like prizes myself.'

'Do you often win them?'

'Not usually. Not now. But I had something the other day that was like a prize to me.'

'Can you tell what it was?'

'It – it was being allowed to join The Group.'

He's lonely, thought Gilly. What a good thing I asked him to join. He's great fun for us, too, being so good at everything and never cross or disagreeable. Perhaps he hasn't a father or a mother. Perhaps he's an orphan. But I'm sure he wouldn't like to be asked. That's the only thing he doesn't like, being asked questions about himself.

The days went by and Brownie became even better established as one of The Group. Once, when Gilly had to be taken to the dentist, they all turned to Brownie for orders, and he invented a wonderful game of cops and robbers that pleased all ages. It became known as Brownie's game.

The other children soon accepted Brownie's strange gift for finding lost objects. If one of the little ones left a sandal on a rock but had no idea which rock, Brownie was quick to say:

'Let's look over there,' or 'try the rock opposite the ice-cream man,' and the sandal was instantly found. He was just as good when the object was a biro or a girl's hair band.

Something told him where to look and the lost article came to light, even if half-buried in the sand. When questioned, he muttered: 'I'm lucky. Some people are.'

One glorious morning, when the sea and the sky were blue and the surface of the bay rippled with little waves, Brownie was not at the meeting place. The Group were amazed. They accepted his presence as inevitable, like Gilly's. They soon made a discovery that worried them even more. Not one of them knew where he was staying.

'I always thought he arrived with you,' said Gilly to the three Ts. 'I'm sure I've seen him with you. I thought he was staying at one of the cottages next to your aunt.'

'We don't know, honestly we don't,' protested Tabby, and Toby and Thomas agreed. 'We've never arrived *with* him, though we're usually early. He's always here first.'

'I somehow thought he was staying at the hotel,' said Nicola. 'No one else is staying there so I thought that was why he's always alone and never waits for anybody.'

'Haven is so small,' said Paula. 'It's silly that we've never wondered where he was staying.'

'It's odd that no one ever came to watch him bathe,' added Marky. 'I thought it was because he swam so well.'

'You see how it is,' said Gilly crossly. 'We all thought this and thought that and thought the other. We never knew anything for certain. We just didn't bother to find out.'

'It didn't seem to matter before, and now it does,' said a quiet boy named Silas. 'I feel we ought to know more. Shall I look in the letter-box? He knew we used it for messages.'

Silas felt down the rabbit hole but only found an empty snail shell.

'We'd better not waste this lovely day,' said Gilly. 'Any ideas?'

They decided to have a beach day, and explore the rocky pools in the morning when the tide was out, and bathe in the afternoon when it would be coming in. They found the

usual anemones and crabs and shrimps, but they all missed
Brownie in different ways. He was always ready to help
anyone who was collecting anything special, though he did
not seem to collect for himself. Sometimes he gathered sea-
weed but always kept it in a pool, not a bucket, and the
tide washed it away as it came in. He once remarked that
that was the idea, though no one knew what he meant.

The day was completely spoilt for Silas because he lost
his new watch on the first day he had ever worn it. It was
his very first watch. He put it in his pocket while he was
dabbling in the pools and it had slipped through a tiny slit
in the lining. They all searched frantically as the tide was
coming in, and Silas's father and mother came to help.
Silas was trying not to cry and kept remembering how his
mother had said: 'Leave it at home till tea-time. It'll be
safer,' and how he'd answered impatiently: 'I know how to

take care of a watch!' He felt very grateful to her for not reminding him of it. He couldn't have borne it if she had.

The rest of The Group were worried too. They knew just how poor Silas was feeling. But there was no sign of the watch and soon it was lunch time with the sea washing over the rocks. Silas didn't want any lunch, but his father said:

'Not eating won't get you anywhere. Come along, now. You'll find that anxiety has made you terribly hungry.'

Gilly wished over and over again that Brownie had been there to help. He had that strange gift of being able to find lost objects. She had a queer feeling that he wasn't far away. That evening, after supper, she slipped out to post a small piece of paper, folded many times, into The Group's letter-box. The paper said:

Brownie, we do need you to find Silas's watch. We all need you. Gilly.

When she got to the sand dunes there was no one about as few people had finished supper. She put her hand down the sandy hole and, to her surprise, found something already there. She took it out, unfolded it and read it several times, though it was a very short letter.

Dear Gilly,
Sorry I couldn't join you this morning, but I had to go back. I may not be able to play with you again but I won't be far away. Try looking for the watch under the wooden steps, the broken ones.

Brownie

It was beautifully written in rather quaint, sloping handwriting.

Gilly thought very quickly. He had had to go back, but back where? But he knew about the lost watch, lost only that very morning. How did he know? How could he

know? Who told him? Or had he, somehow, seen them searching? It was a warm, windless evening, but Gilly shivered. There was something here that she did not understand and she knew she never would.

She never doubted that she would find the watch just where he said. There were two short flights of rickety wooden steps down on to the beach, one more broken than the other. Everyone simply jumped down, so they were never repaired. She walked back to the broken ones and there was the watch, just as it had fallen between the wooden planks forming the treads. It was still going.

Gilly called at the cottage where Silas was staying and gave him the watch, and he and his parents were too pleased and excited to wonder why she had looked just there.

'I know,' said Silas. 'I went back for my net and I expect I jumped down the steps as I always do, and the jump jolted the watch out. It's still ticking and says exactly the right time.' He compared it with the clock on the mantelpiece.

The warmth and satisfaction over the watch brought Gilly back to the real world where things were lost and found, and people belonged together in families. This was her world, even if it wasn't Brownie's and could never be.